Slocum ... ...him came all the wide-eyed customers in the place who'd hurried to finish their drink so they wouldn't miss a blow. His eye on the enemy, Slocum handed a man in the crowd his felt hat.

"Queensbury rules?" he asked. The crowd laughed.

"Hell, we don't need no rules," Hubbard said, sparring with his fists to loosen himself up. "Man can't get up, then it's over."

Hubbard came scuffling over, made a wild swing, and Slocum drove a barrage of fists into his gut. The gunslinger danced away from two, then three of the big man's wild punches and made two of his own to Hubbard's face that drew a shocked expression.

"Stand still or I'll kill you!" Hubbard growled, wading in for a lucky hit.

"You said no rules."

Hubbard telegraphed his next try.

The haymaker missed Slocum's face by inches. But the gunslinger's right swing drove his knuckles into Hubbard's temple and stunned the big man. Slocum never missed a chance and drove in with hard blows to the man's gut, barely escaping an arm.

"Damn you!" Hubbard's voice was a roar like a mad grizzly and he came, guard down, to get ahold of Slocum. His mistake—one, two, three punches to the head drove back his attack. The big man wobbled on his feet and Slocum drove in, his hands aching with each hit until Hubbard's knees buckled.

The man's whore screamed, "No!"

DON'T MISS THESE
ALL-ACTION WESTERN SERIES
FROM THE BERKLEY PUBLISHING GROUP

THE GUNSMITH by J. R. Roberts
Clint Adams was a legend among lawmen, outlaws, and ladies.
They called him . . . the Gunsmith.

LONGARM by Tabor Evans
The popular long-running series about Deputy U.S. Marshal
Long—his life, his loves, his fight for justice.

SLOCUM by Jake Logan
Today's longest-running action Western. John Slocum rides
a deadly trail of hot blood and cold steel.

BUSHWHACKERS by B. J. Lanagan
An action-packed series by the creators of Longarm! The
rousing adventures of the most brutal gang of cutthroats ever
assembled—Quantrill's Raiders.

DIAMONDBACK by Guy Brewer
Dex Yancey is Diamondback, a Southern gentleman turned
con man when his brother cheats him out of the family fortune. Ladies love him. Gamblers hate him. But nobody pulls
one over on Dex . . .

WILDGUN by Jack Hanson
The blazing adventures of mountain man Will Barlow—from
the creators of Longarm!

TEXAS TRACKER by Tom Calhoun
Meet J. T. Law: the most relentless—and dangerous—man-
hunter in all Texas. Where sheriffs and posses fail, he's the
best man to bring in the most vicious outlaws—for a price.

JAKE LOGAN

SLOCUM

AND THE CAYUSE SQUAW

JOVE BOOKS, NEW YORK

This is a work of fiction. Names, characters, places, and incidents either are the product of the author's imagination or are used fictitiously, and any resemblance to actual persons, living or dead, business establishments, events, or locales is entirely coincidental.

SLOCUM AND THE CAYUSE SQUAW

A Jove Book / published by arrangement with
the author

PRINTING HISTORY
Jove edition / March 2004

Copyright © 2004 by Penguin Group (USA) Inc.

For information address: The Berkley Publishing Group,
a division of Penguin Group (USA) Inc.,
375 Hudson Street, New York, New York 10014.

ISBN: 0-515-13697-2

A JOVE BOOK®
Jove Books are published by The Berkley Publishing Group,
a division of Penguin Group (USA) Inc.,
375 Hudson Street, New York, New York 10014.
JOVE and the "J" design
are trademarks belonging to Penguin Group (USA) Inc.

PRINTED IN THE UNITED STATES OF AMERICA

10 9 8 7 6 5 4 3 2 1

1

He reined up the hard-breathing dun horse. His mane unfurled in the wind, the lathered animal bent over and snorted in the dust, then like a shot the dun threw its head up in Wayne's face. But neither the horse he contained by the reins in his fist nor the mustang herd galloping away from him across the purple sagebrush held the man's interest. Minutes before in hot pursuit of the bangtails, from the side of his vision he'd caught sight of something suspicious down by the creek. Perhaps an illusion, perhaps not, but he swore he'd seen the flash of a skirt in those thick willows across the stream.

Standing in the stirrups, he studied the dense growth beyond the shallow stream. When he glanced back to check on the wild ones with mixed emotions about what to do next, the mustangs were already a mile ahead of him. Their dust rose like a waving column of smoke against the azure sky. Be no horses in the trap this day. That would be all right—especially if his eyes had not deceived him. The notion of a female only yards away made his guts churn, and the manhood in his pants stiffened at the thought.

How long had it been since he'd had any? Three, four months—the last time was back in the winter, anyway. Out of desperation, he'd stomped up the worn staircase over Kelsey's bar and paid four bits for ten lousy minutes rutting that fat sow, Morine. Kelsey kept her upstairs, because she was so goddamn ugly, she'd run off customers hanging around in the bar.

Man had to be plumb drunk and horny as a billy goat to even consider mounting her big white ass. She smelled worse than a hog. Her musk about gagged him and she used lots of cheap perfume that only made the stench worse.

"You ever took a bath, Morine?" he asked her.

"Christ sakes, yes. You're the second dumb prick asked me that this week. I took one when it got warm last spring."

"Last spring? Ah, for God's sake, why did you even bother then?"

" 'Cause," she said, being coy as any flabby three-hundred-pound elephant could act. "You need at least two baths a year."

"How the hell do you stand the expense of the soap and water?"

"Jeez, you come to do business with your poker or to palaver your head off all day? It's cold up here, and if you ain't getting in bed with me, I'm putting some clothes back on."

"Hold onto your horses, I'll be there." He hurriedly undressed. The deep chill of the room swept his skin and hastened the process. No damn heat upstairs. If he wasn't pretty well loaded, he'd never have considered climbing them steep steps. Then he heard a loud thumping on the floor under them.

"What the hell is that?" he asked, putting his knees on the edge of the rope bed.

"Get under the goddamn blankets and get busy. I've got me another one waiting—that's Kelsey giving me the signal."

"Ah, shit!"

"Don't ah-shit me, get your poker in me and get to humping, you hatchet-assed Texan." She held the blankets up like a tent until he climbed over her huge sausage leg. Him between them, she dropped the bedcovers over him and laid on her back looking at the ceiling like a dead sow. "Get on with it. I ain't got all day."

Under the warm sun, his shoulders gave a shudder and

goose bumps ran up the back of his arms under the sleeves of his shirt, thinking about that day. He could have fucked a sheep as well as her. Might have been better. Intent on finding what he'd seen a few minutes earlier, he kept studying the waving, head-high willows for any more sign of her.

Filled with impatience, he spurred the dun down the steep bank of white volcanic ash. If there was a female there, he'd find her. What the hell was one doing out there anyway? No ranches in this end of the valley. No sign of some honyocker's wagon. Who in the hell could she be? If it wasn't his imagination playing tricks on him—he'd find her.

The stout dun he called Bob splashed knee-deep through Crab Creek, and he sent him into the thicket of twisting willows. Once they were inside, he was forced to separate the branches as Bob pushed his way through the tangled stems that were thick as hair. Wayne fought them away and pushed on. Damn, a female could hide from an army in this stuff. Then they broke into a small clearing and Wayne grinned at the sight of the ragged canvas stretched over a willow-branch lodge. A fire under an iron pot, some Injun things scattered about—no dream, no illusion.

He reached down insides his pants and made his hard-on point straight up, so it didn't break off. He chuckled with the excitement growing inside his brain over his discovery. The next thing was where had she gone? Then young or old? She couldn't be any worse than Morine—a sourness rose in back of his tongue at the thought of Kelsey's enormous pig. This one would have to have maggots in her crotch to be that bad.

He dismounted heavily. His spurs gave a ring and he undid his bull-hide batwing chaps to hang them over the saddle horn. Lot of cowboys up in the Northwest wore those wooly ones, but he still liked his better. All he was ever used to, all they ever wore in Texas. Why, a guy showed up in San Angelo, Waco, San Antonio wearing them woolly things, he'd get laughed out of town.

Shame after he shot that trail boss on the San Antonio Square over that dark-eyed *puta,* he had to hightail it out of there for the hill country, and after the next ruckus head back for his family's country in Missouri.

He wiped his whisker-bristled lips on the side of his index finger. Where did she go? Why, he hated this north country as bad as Missouri. There were *putas* all over Texas. Little Latin darlings, good-looking and hotter than any bitch in heat. What did they have up here—rawboned women and fat slobs. They must have got the ugly ones rounded up back east and put them all on a wagon train for Washington and Oregon. The one he had in Yule City couldn't even talk English—maybe Norwegian. She was square-shouldered as a man—had a nose long as a carrot and her tits were flat as pancakes. Still charged him a dollar—by God, she knew money even if she couldn't speak any damn English.

He took off his felt hat and scratched his head. In this damn windy country, he had to wear a hat string or lose it. Shame, he couldn't go back to Texas—no way after that shoot-out in Kirksville. He gunned down two deputies and put enough lead into Sheriff Randal Iverson, they had to reenforce the casket to keep him from falling out of the bottom. No account trash, they had it coming. They'd shot down his brother Alfred a week before, for no good reason at all. Anyway, he got his revenge for Al.

He glanced at the sun. Past noon. Where was this squaw at? She couldn't be too ugly after all he had been through. His wife he married at the end of the war, got her knocked up twice in two years—boy and girl—but he couldn't stand her all the time nagging him so he went off to Texas and made cattle drives for a few years. After all that shooting business, he went back to Joplin and found a pretty cousin, Charlene. Man, she was all right.

Searching for the female along the gurgling stream, he kept thinking about Charlene. This along with catching a glimpse of a female had him upset. He shoved his hand in behind his belt and straightened up his rod again. Getting hornier by the minute.

"Come here, darling. I've got something for you," he shouted, then threw his head back, feeling filled with the power of a stallion, and laughed out loud. But only the wind in the tossing willows answered him. He swung in the saddle and decided to ride out the thicket some more. Maybe he could flush her out.

In minutes, he came to the end of the greenery and emerged into the sagebrush sea. His heart stopped at the sight of her. A figure in a buckskin-fringed skirt was struggling to climb the rise. She looked back at him, and then with a toss of her shoulder-length braids, she began to run again.

"Heeyah!" he screamed at Bob. The dun lurched forward and headed for Wayne's escaping prize. Pounding hooves thundered across the ground, spur rowels driving him harder. Wayne bent over in the saddle when he got aside her, then reached out for her shoulders and dove out of his seat. His arms closed around her and his weight sent them both face-first into the brittle sage. Bob thundered away.

A brief struggle and he overpowered her, forcing her on her back on the ground with him astraddle of her stomach. Injun bitch! Her dark eyes were in slits as he gloated over his find. He pinned her arms down over her head until he had both her hands held in his left hand, then he reached down and ripped apart her rotten leather blouse. He smiled at the sight of her pear-shaped breasts.

"You ready for some screwing?" he asked, short of breath from his efforts. "I'm going to screw your ass off, you little bitch. Whew, this is too damn good to be true.

"Girl, you savvy English?"

No response. She bored holes in him with her dark eyes.

"Guess you don't—don't need to, all you need to do is spread them legs and let me in there."

No answer. She strained to escape but was no match for his superior strength and weight.

"You a virgin? Godamighty, I couldn't be that lucky." He looked around—she have anyone with her? Hell, he might get his hair lifted—if'n he wasn't more careful. Why was she alone? Feeling eerie about the entire deal, he twisted to look for signs of anyone.

Wasn't like Injuns being alone. Nothing in sight. He removed his gunbelt and tossed it aside. Seeing Bob, his head down grazing, made him feel better about his security. If Bob noticed anyone or thing, he'd raise up and stare. Horses made better sentries than dogs for jobs like that if you watched them. They never missed a thing. Saved him several times from being snuck up on.

He smiled down at her, his concerns of their being alone settled. Reckon she knew what he was going to do to her? "Look as mad at me as you want, girl—I got this big hard-on that's going up your snatch."

Oh, he could hardly breathe, his heart ran so fast. He pushed off his galluses, and opened his pants still astraddle her. No underwear. His erection sprung out like a sapling and her eyes flew open at the sight of the shiny, pink phallus in the bright sunlight.

"That's it," he bragged.

She exploded and he found himself riding a wild bronc. Tossed aside, he reached for her skirt as she scrambled to get to her feet, but his fingers missed the hem by inches. Forced to hold up his pants, he tore after her, closing his pants and putting up a suspender as he went. Her long dress slowed her some. In ten strides, he dove for her and came up with an armful of legs and material.

She frantically undid the ties at her waist, kicking and squirming as he tried to secure her, and in an instant a leather skirt was all he grasped. A flash of her brown legs getting away from him, and she was up and running again. With a roar of anger, he jumped to his feet, shoved one gallus over his shoulder to hold up his pants and took off to catch her again.

Her bare copper limbs reached out in long strides. She soon began to outdistance him. He could see the twin moons of her shapely brown butt, but no way he'd ever overtake her as she ran unrestricted.

His heart threatening to burst, he headed back for Bob. Only on horse back could he ever catch her. Breath gone, legs aching, he caught the dun, leaped in the saddle and headed him after the fleeing girl.

How old was she? Fifteen, maybe sixteen. She could be a virgin. What the hell was she doing out there all alone? Hell, he hadn't seen any Injuns in this country since the past fall. Then they'd been spearing and drying salmon down on the Columbia, way west of his mustang-chasing country. Her dark eyes wide with fear when she glanced over her shoulder at him, she headed for the creek. He spurred Bob in that direction.

The dun dodged sagebrush as he sent him down the slope. She looked back, panic written on her face, and plunged into the water. Bob made three good lunges and Wayne dove off the saddle to take her down in the water. Under they went in the knee-deep stream and both came up sputtering.

Ahold of one arm, he dragged her, kicking and squalling, to the grassy bank. At last there, he dropped his galluses, knelt down and roughly pushed aside her flailing wet legs. Her brown limbs spread apart and her womanhood exposed, he swiftly moved in to fill the void with his shaft before she could squeeze him out. He guided his aching dick into her gates and gave a big hunch. His taut-skinned tool entered her tight walls, and his aching butt began to thrust him into her. He pinned her shoulders down with his hands and glared at her as the pleasure began to make his head swarm.

"I got you now. Boy, you've got a tight pussy. You got a man?" Then he saw the rage in her dark eyes melt as he put the meat to her some more. Harder, faster. Damn her brown ass, he knew she'd like it. They all did when you got it stuck up in them. His breath rasping out of his sore throat, knives in his lungs, he savored her muscular walls and pumped his swollen, tight dick into her. At last, he felt the end coming and drove his stick home. He cried out as he came inside her like a giant rocket bursting in the sky.

"You must be a damn Cayuse," he said, exhausted and sitting up on his heels. The fight was gone from her. She looked bleary eyed when she raising herself up on her elbows.

"Thought you're one of them. You must have been a damn virgin. Look there, I got blood all over my dick and me." He made a face at the mess on his privates.

She shook her head in disgust at his condition; then she took the side of her hand and slid it over her throat.

"Who you doing that to?" he demanded, noticing a strong

smell and then scenting his hand. What was that? She having her time of the month, too?

She pointed at her crotch, then at him and made the same sign again.

"What're you getting at girl? You saying your bloody pussy's going to kill me?" He frowned hard at her for an answer.

She made a ring with one finger and pushed a finger from the other hand through it, then pointed at him.

"Yeah, I savvy that. Me—I screwed you." He nodded; he knew what she meant.

Then she pointed at the drying blood on his privates.

"Yeah, you were a virgin. Me number one?" He held up his finger in her face.

She shook her head.

"Where did all the damn blood come from?" He looked at her and smiled. Hell, he could do it again. He began to tug on his manhood and it responded.

He motioned for her lay back down. "This may kill me like you say, but I'll be damned if it ain't nice. Lay back down. I want to do this again."

She shook her head in disapproval, but she obeyed him this time.

Three days later, he thought he had had all the pussy he could take for one man. She'd stopped bleeding every time they did it and his mind went back to catching some mustangs. He called her "Squaw" and she cooked the rabbits and grouse he shot with a .22 and fixed him beans. He hadn't seen any deer close enough to kill lately, but he had promised her one. Though he doubted she understood him. She never spoke a word to him—either dumb or just stubborn. He didn't bother worrying about it much.

All he knew about her origin he could put in a tobacco sack. He did know how to stick his dick in her tight pussy, and that was about the total case. With his own new silent plaything, he tried it up, down and even from behind. Damn brown bitch was sure better ass than his wife, who always acted like screwing was awful or sinful. Squaw had even begun to show she enjoyed it near as well as his cousin Charlene had when he was with her.

The next seven months were like heaven for Wayne out there on the sagebrush sea. He spent most of the winter laid up with her in a cot, screwing her under a pile of warm blankets. He simply couldn't get enough of her. Word was out in town, he was a squaw man. Someone must have seen her in his camp. He didn't give a fuck what they saw. They asked him lots of questions when he periodically went to town to sell some ponies he broke out or to get more supplies. None of their business, that he had him a woman with a red ass—that was his choosing. She was getting kind of big by then with child, but it still was fun diddling her. Damn her hard ass, though, she never spoke a word, and he liked that for the most part. White women drove him crazy nagging all the time. Hell, he'd left his wife over her complaining every waking hour about something, and Charlene wasn't much better.

His wife was dead of consumption and that damn bitch Charlene found her a sugar daddy in St. Charles. And one day he discovered this brown screwing machine in the Washington desert under the Mustang Mountains. The notion brought a sly smile to his whiskered face.

As he rode in the warming spring sunshine, trailing a band of mustangs, it still made him dizzy headed to even think about rubbing bellies with the naked Squaw. He hoped to head the mustangs into his trap by some spooks he'd put up to divert their usual pattern. His spooks consisted of greasy tow sacks strung across the way the horses usually ran. Supposed to turn them aside and up the canyon for his trap.

The lead mare proved to be a caution, and he had considered killing her with his .44–40 Winchester. Too damn smart. But this time as he rode up the valley behind them in a long lope, she turned and at the last minute sucked back from the sacks. Then she plunged into the side canyon, headed for the trap with two dozen others on her heels. Filled with the excitement of his success, Wayne came off the mountainside after them whooping like a Comanche.

By God, he'd have him a half dozen head of good ones

out of the drive this time. He was counting the gold, when Bob stumbled and went down. The force of his fall sent the unsuspecting Wayne sailing out over the dun's head. Arms outstretched, he went facedown onto the steep hillside, sliding in the loose ash. The force of the fall sent the dun flipping end over end. Bob's shadow fell on Wayne in the instant the flying horse was poised above him. Too late, the disarranged Wayne tried hopelessly to ward off the impact of the horse's body falling on top of him.

Crushed under the thousand pounds of horse and saddle that landed on him, he lay pinned beneath the weight of the fallen gelding, who struggled, trying to get up. Wayne recalled the sight of her showing him a brown finger going through the ring of the other one and the side of her hand like a knife crossing her throat. *The bitch got her way.*

Crushed—and he knew from the hard pain, he must be broken up real bad inside. Wayne died slowly in the bright afternoon sun, not easy, but alone, save a dun horse standing hipshot nearby and some ravens who cried to the wind about his demise.

2

Red-orange gunshots flared in the night from across the dark street. Slocum tried to make out the whereabouts of the second bounty hunter. Crouched behind the rain barrel, he saved the last three bullets in his Colt for "good" targets. They'd overplayed their hand or he'd have been a captured man only seconds before when they accosted him on the porch of the saloon.

"You see him?" the first one shouted to the other.

"Naw, the sumbitch is somewhere across the street from you."

"You move to the right and I'll watch for him."

"Yeah and get my ass shot off. That bastard's armed. No way."

"He can't have many bullets left."

More than they thought. Taking cartridges from his belt, Slocum finished reloading his Colt, then twisted around and looked down the inky, narrow passageway between the two buildings. He needed a horse and a way out of this burg. Where in the hell those two came from he had no idea. They'd jumped him coming out of the saloon . . .

"Hold everything," someone ordered. "I'm the law here. Marshal Thomas."

"Marshal, glad you came, but we've got us a Kansas killer right over there."

"Hold that damn shooting—"

11

Enough was enough. In a low crouch Slocum headed for the back alley. The smell of spent gunpowder in his nose, he reached the back of the buildings, paused, listened and heard no pursuit—only the lawman, out in front, still shouting for everyone to hold their fire. The smell of rotten refuse replaced the sulfurous gunpowder odor in his nose. With a little starlight to guide him, he scattered a dozen cats in a half run up the path until he was behind the livery.

He eased himself inside the back door. The strong winy smell of horse piss filled his nostrils when he paused, checking his hard breathing, and turned his ear for any sounds of pursuit. Horses chomped on hay and others stomped in their sleep. He needed one that was saddled. That would be sheer luck—unless someone had left one for just a few hours, not trusting it to stay hitched while they were in a bar having a few drinks or frequenting some cathouse. Against the dim lantern light that shone from the front, Slocum spotted a saddle horn sticking up. Easing his way past the butts of various animals toward the one under the rig, he paused once with his shoulder against a post to consider his next move. His breathing easier by then, he moved swiftly toward his goal.

In the tie stall, he spoke softly to the horse, checked the cinch and, satisfied it was tight enough, backed the animal out into the alleyway. The stout horse blew rollers out his nose like he might have some buck in him. There'd be no time for any foolishness.

Then he heard the clatter of boot heels on the boardwalk, coming in his direction. Damn, one of them was headed his way. He cheeked the horse by his headstall to keep the horse's head close to his leg when he mounted him. His intentions were to charge out the open doorway and get the hell out of this little place and as far away as possible from those two bounty men.

"Heeyah," he squalled, and ducked low over the saddle, Colt in his right hand. The bay burst into the dark street. Slocum fired a snap shot to his left where he suspected the runner would be by the time he passed through the doorway. Then he swung the gelding to the right, driving him up the inky street, lashing the big horse from side to side with the reins.

Shots rang out behind him. A burning bee stung his left shoulder and he knew they'd gotten lucky. He holstered his Colt and switched hands with the reins. The big horse needed no more encouragement. A numbing pain in his left shoulder blade told Slocum he needed lots of distance between him and those reward seekers.

They'd pursue him, too. He needed to think about that. The ground-gaining gait of the big horse felt good between his legs, but for how long and how far could he stand it? Needed to circle back west. They'd be on the telegraph to every whistle stop to the east in a matter of minutes. That was unless they were real selfish. Then they'd not want to lose or divide the reward with some hayseed town law. Greed might work to his advantage—but he couldn't count on it.

Yard dogs barked at him when he passed dark homesteads. He brought the big gelding down to a long trot under the star-speckled ceiling. They still had many miles ahead of them that night, and he sure didn't need to run him into the ground. If only he knew the pairs' faces better. They weren't the usual outfit on his heels—the two Abbott Brothers. He knew those two Kansas deputies on sight and their voices as well. How this pair recognized him was another mystery— the poster's description fit a thousand men. They evidently knew something more and must have dogged him there.

The crack of dawn found him westward bound in a sagebrush sea bordered by two ranges of hills. His shirt stuck to his back with the dried blood. The wound felt like a war lance, and the shake of the ride made him think the long shaft was wobbling over him.

Green willows down the center of the basin told him there might be water down there. A check over his shoulder showed no sign of pursuit, but how far could he see? They would come. He needed some kind of hideout—sanctuary. Nothing but knee-high sage and bunchgrass. Wincing at the sharpness of his wound, he drew a ragged breath. Be a hell of a place to die—somewhere in eastern Washington. Hadn't seen a cow brute, only some signs of wild mustangs—old horse apples and tracks. The honyockers weren't even in this part of the country yet. East of there, they'd already grubbed up thousands of acres of sagebrush to plant wheat.

He used the saddle horn to steady himself. No time to get light headed. Maybe a drink at that stream would help him. Then he tried to assess his condition and strength. Could he remount the horse if he got off?

The water sparkled like silver when he drew up the bay. With measured deep breathing, he eased himself out of the saddle. Dizzy headed, and wobbly on his boot heels, he led the bay to the edge of the sandbar and dropped the reins.

The gelding put down his head and began to slurp up his needs. Slocum fell to his knees, recovered, then bent face-down. He stuck his head half under and let the water cool his cheeks and the rest. Raising up, he found his activity caused the fire in his shoulder to increase. On his hands and knees, water dripping from his face, refreshing it, he reached out to capture the reins.

With a snort, the bay spooked sideways and jerked them away from his grasp. Filled with the shocking knowledge that if he couldn't catch them he'd be afoot in this desolate country, he moved slower toward the boogered horse, who showed lots of white around his eyes.

"Easy—easy," Slocum coaxed, fighting to get to his feet. He read this newfound fear in the bay's eyes—his only opportunity to recover him lay in the fact the horse wasn't convinced that he was free yet. Slocum knew how thin his chances were in his weakened condition of ever getting ahold of the trailing leather.

"Whoa, big man," he coaxed, on his feet at last. He pushed off his upper leg to straighten.

The gelding sidled toward the sage. With some effort he moved after the bay, Slocum's hand held out as if with an offering. He talked softly to the leery horse, knowing full well his own life hung in the balance of his success or failure. One eye shut to help close out the gnawing fire in his back, he swallowed hard and let out an exhale.

Then behind the horse something exploded out of the sage. Wild eyed as if goosed, the bay started and threw his head up. Slocum made a desperate rush for the escaping reins and fell facedown, then reached hard—and came up with nothing in his fingers. A prairie chicken—the bay had flushed him. Slocum grimaced listening to the thundering hooves of the gelding headed back toward town. Sand in his mouth, he lay belly down, spitting the grit and closing his eyes. The bay was gone. Only the drumbeat of his hooves growing fainter was left.

He would never have found a saddled horse in the livery if he hadn't been a spook. A risk he knew when he took him. Oh, well, they'd have a hard time hanging a rustling charge on him. The evidence was headed home.

New predicament—those bounty hunters might be able to backtrack him. Damn, he wished he could think clear. All they had to do was follow the gelding's hoofprints to find him. Better get up and shake that trail. The creek ran west. It should lead somewhere, to more water, bigger? He drew a deep breath for strength and pushed himself to his feet; then, holding his left arm to his body, he set out climbing the bank so his tracks wouldn't be so obvious. At last, he looked back to the east and thought he could see the fleeing bay. His mane unfurled, head high, racing like a free mustang. He was savoring his escape in a wild charge through the smelly sage. Damn him.

Slocum was unsure how far he staggered westward. Night and day became a mixture—until all his strength expired. When his knees buckled, he collapsed, passed out—and awoke dumb, numb, searched for the North Star, got up and trudged on like a man half-dead. Hunger pains came and passed. Stumbling around in a daze, he wasn't sure about going the wrong way some of the time. But he stayed close and watered in the meandering creek. Somewhere he'd lost his hat—couldn't recall when or where. He looked about for it—found nothing. The sun blinded him, forced him to squint at the purple hills.

Tired, dizzy, needed to rest—sleep awhile. He crossed the creek searching for a place to lie down in the shade. He slugged through the water, filling his boots. Sloshing on in the sodden footgear, he climbed the bank, fell facedown and didn't wake until someone shook him.

"Huh?" He blinked at her. Looking up, he saw the shocked face of an Indian girl with a papoose. He guessed her age at perhaps sixteen–eighteen. Young anyway.

She pointed to her shoulder.

"Yeah, they shot me." He didn't recognize his own gravely voice and gazed in disbelief at her through his fuzzy vision. She didn't understand a word he'd said. He could see nothing registered on her handsome long brown face.

"Who're you?" He pointed at her.

"Cayuse."

That meant horse up in that country. Sign language—he'd done it with Comanches, might work with a Cayuse. Lying on his side, he tried to get where he could use his hands. She edged closer until she was squatted only a few feet from him. He could smell her, a woman's musk—a milky smell for she must nurse the baby—and wood smoke. Her eyes narrowed when he began using his fingers to build words.

He made the sign for "I am hurt."

She nodded and swung the papoose down to set it on the ground. Quickly she folded her legs under her and began to respond to him with her fingers.

"How can I help?"

"I need a bullet dug out of my back." He did it over, anxious for her to understand his signs.

She shook her head like he'd asked too much of her. Looking distrustful at him, she held up her hands and he could see the pain in her face. He took out his jackknife and opened it. Restricted by his position, he began to probe with point of the blade in the dirt. He dug out a small stone with the tip and showed it to her between two fingers.

More hand signs for her. "I need the bullet out."

Indecision in her brown eyes, she looked taken aback by the whole thing. Her head shake was one of no-I-can't-do-that.

"You can do it. Build a fire and we will heat the knife. You build a small fire."

She nodded with an eye to the baby—then as if satisfied

the little fellow was all right there with him, she signaled back. "Me—build small fire."

He bobbed his head in agreement. His skull pounded with a headache, but he rose to his knees in the darkness of his vision to watch her gather dead sage, and she soon came back with an armload.

He dug some matches out of his pocket and she nodded with enthusiasm. In minutes, she had the small, pungent fire going. He held the blade over the flame. She went behind him and he felt her touch the shirt. Maybe she would get the bullet out.

Then she pushed his galluses off his shoulders and came to kneel before him. She reached for the buttons down the front. He nodded and she cautiously began to unbutton them. Once the shirt was undone, she eased it over his shoulder, then with care worked it off him, peeling it gently away from where the dried blood stuck it to his skin. Soon he realized she'd removed it. Wind swept his bare torso. She got up and ran to the creek for a handful of water.

He shook his head at her when she started back; then he pointed he would go there. His teeth clenched tight, he staggered to his feet with her at his side to steady him. The effort sapped his strength. He fell to his knees beside the clear water. With a piece torn from his shirt for a rag in her hands, she took great care to wash his back. Some cold liquid ran down into his waistband. No matter.

Then she took his good arm and helped him up to move to a place higher. He sprawled facedown on the short grass bank. She squatted at her small fire and heated the blade of his knife. He closed his eyes to steel himself for what came next when she returned. Soon he felt the point scratch the ball in his shoulder. Teeth clenched tight, he forced himself to endure the pain as the point probed into the muscles to unseat the missile. He knew he couldn't scream, though he wanted to—it might scare her from the task. Then the pain shot through his upper body like a bolt of lightning. His mouth flew open and in the distance he heard his own cry and fainted.

He awoke. His shoulder felt on fire. Across from him, he

could see her sitting cross-legged and nursing the small baby. She smiled and held up her fingers with a small bullet to show him she got it out. He nodded in gratitude and she went back to suckling the child. Lots for him to comprehend and consider: how he ever was moved, for he began to realize that he was inside a tent, on a cot. There was a camelback trunk, a rimfire saddle, some ropes, someone's hat. Where was her man?

"Where is he?" he asked her in sign.

"Dead" was the signal.

He nodded he understood, then he lay back facedown on the cot—out of breath. She got to her feet and hung the papoose on a tent pole. He wasn't about to argue with her. She had packed his wound with something and he had to accept it was adequate. The bleeding had stopped. Unable to keep his eyes open any longer, he fell back asleep.

She woke him later and had some tea-like brew in a tin cup. Still uncertain about her name, he sat on the edge of the bed and considered his state. Damn near defenseless. His Colt was all that was left. No horse and weak as a pup. Tough place to be in if he had not been befriended by her. The tea tasted funny, but he accepted her effort in good faith.

"Your name?" He made sign.

"Cayuse."

"No." He pointed at her. "Your name."

"Squaw, me Squaw," she said aloud.

He nodded, pleased she could talk. The guy who owned this gear called her that. Shame he had no more imagination than that for the poor woman's name.

"How did your man die?" he asked, grateful she wasn't mute. Her voice sounded melodious to him. He wanted her to talk a lot more.

"Horse fall on him."

"Oh. You have no one?"

She pointed at him and then at herself. "You—me—we make big mustangers."

For a second, he considered her offer. Then he nodded, not wishing to offend her at all. How they would capture mustangs on foot he had no idea, but her proposal sounded sincere enough. He recalled the bay's escape and realized yet again he didn't have a horse. A mustang would be a way to get out of there—give him mobility.

"We catch mustang," he said, relieved that she could talk some English.

A smile crossed her copper face. She drew her head back with pride. Then she rose and took the papoose down again to feed it. The little baby acted pleased and made loud noises when she placed him at her breast.

"What's the baby's name?"

"Wine." She looked hard at him, as if questioning her word.

"Wayne?"

She nodded in approval and looked down at her papoose.

That must have been her dead man's name. He searched around the tent. The sunlight filtered through the canvas, casting a yellow light in the interior. Very neat place. Considering the surroundings in the tent, the interior was trash free. Highly unlikely looking for an Indian camp or even a white man's place. How long had her man been dead? No telling.

Then he heard horses and rose to his sea legs, gun in his hand. She scrambled to her feet and shook her head in disapproval. Indicating for him to stay back with a serious frown, she ducked and went out the flap with her baby. Pistol in hand, he stood far enough back so they couldn't see him or his shadow on the material sides.

"We're looking for a white man," a demanding voice outside said.

3

Slocum eased back the hammer on the .44. His ear turned to hear every word spoken outside the tent. He wished he could see the men confronting her out in front of the flaps.

"Where the hell is your man, squaw?"

"Goddamn her, she deaf?" Then the unmistakable sounds of an impatient horse circling around. Slocum listened, ready to bust outside to her rescue at the first sign of any physical threat to her.

"Him mustang."

"Goddamn squaw man. It's got so he don't come to town much anymore. Guess he figured he ain't welcome there. Him out here rutting with you and making them damn breed pickaninnies, huh?"

"Him mustanging."

"Yeah, girl, we heard you. You seen anyone else? A white man on a big bay horse?"

"All she's seen is the ceiling of that tent when her man comes home." The man laughed aloud. "I could use me a little of that Injun pussy, myself. Come on, she don't know nothing. We're burning daylight."

"Where in the hell has this Slocum gone—"

"He'll turn up again. We'll be ready to go and find him."

"Somebody better tell that Marvin Reagan that sumbitch stole his damn bay horse and got away with it."

"Let's get back to town. Slocum's not out here."

"You boys go ahead—me and this Cayuse bitch got us some business to tend to."

"Her old man Wayne Coats comes back and catches you diddling her, he might blow that dick of yours plumb off for messing with her."

"Hmm. She ain't half-bad to look at."

"Goddammit, come on. There's better-looking white girls at Shelley's than that."

"Ward, you ain't no damn judge of good-looking women. I seen you screwing hogs in Idaho in that logging camp."

"Boys, ain't neither of you messing with that Cayuse squaw."

"Why? You a damn Injun lover, Marshal?"

"Hell no, Carter, I hate the damn red boogers bad as any man, but we better leave her alone. I don't need no trouble with Injuns on my part."

Carter and Ward? Who in the hell were they? The names meant nothing to Slocum, and he'd had no clear look at them in the dark during the saloon porch confrontation. One of them he recalled wore a mustache. Standing at the tent flap, he watched their backs riding off. The black suit must belong to the marshal, Thomas. The gray hats on the bounty men were high-crowned. One wore a leather vest; the other wore a gray wool one and rode a pale dun horse he thought he could recognize again. The leather-vested bounty man was on board a nondescript bay.

"No-good—" She swept by him coming in the tent, carrying the papoose, anger in her brown eyes, the mouth set in a hard line.

"You know them?"

She whirled and blinked at him.

He repeated the words in sign language.

She shook her head and spit out her words. "Think Squaw's a whore for all white men."

"Who taught you English?"

"Learn some trader. Some school."

"You don't speak it much."

"Not talk it good. White men make fun of me."

"Wayne make fun of your English?"

"No," she spat out. "Me never ever speak to him in English."

He stared at her in disbelief. "You never said a word to him. Not once?"

She shook her head and then her hard look softened and she grinned. "Him make me so mad." Her braids were dancing with fury as she made clenched fist at her side and stomped her moccasins on the ground. "Made me him wife. Me no want him."

"What happened?" Slocum frowned at her.

"Me away from camp. He see me. Run me down with horse and make me him wife."

"You never ever spoke to Wayne?" he asked, still not believing her.

She shook her head. "Him *nicky-do* me at bad time, too."

Slocum nodded. Indians were superstitious about menses. Women went into seclusion during their periods. Obviously this mustanger had not recognized her condition in his haste to rape her.

"How long has he been dead?"

"Four–five moons."

"No wonder they ain't seen him. You bury him?"

She nodded. "Me look and look for him. No horse. Him no leave me one. 'Fraid me run away. Me walk with big belly." She indicated her condition with her hands. "Not go fast. Look lots of places. Me find him dead. Horse fall on him." She went to the doorway and pointed toward the line of hills in the south to where she must have found his corpse.

"You know those men that were here today?"

She shook her head. "No. Them bad white men."

"Why did you help me?"

She turned her pale palms up at him. "No bad things in your eyes."

"You looked at me, good?"

"Look plenty good." She swept up the papoose, opened the blouse to expose her pointed breast and began to let him nurse. "Why they want you?"

"Old deal. A boy was shot. His father never accepted he was armed and coming for me."

"Blood deal?" she asked, switching the baby to the other side and holding up the breast for him to take.

"Blood deal. Where are your people?"

"With Nez Percé." She shrugged. "They got plenty wormy flour. Plenty tough beef to eat there. A few Cayuse came here to find a place to spear fish. I come along."

"They go back?"

She nodded. "Told them go home. I must stay after he make me his wife. No want any trouble with whites. Might bring soldiers. My people die."

"Where is the fish river?" He knew she meant the Columbia.

"Two days' ride." She pointed to the west.

"You been chasing mustangs by yourself?"

"When baby can ride on my back." She beamed at him and straightened herself with a newfound pride.

"What if your horse falls like his did?"

She shrugged away his concern. "Being white man's squaw bad deal—no man's squaw bad deal, too."

"Why not join your people?"

"Who wants white man's castoff?" She nodded to the papoose. "Me catch many fine horses, then go home. They never say thing, when I got plenty horses."

"How many will it take?"

"Many, two moons."

"Forty, fifty?"

She nodded and smiled big. "Fifty be plenty good."

He went to the front of the tent and studied the rolling purple sea. Fifty captured wild mustangs would be a lot of horses to gather. Gentled enough to stay in a herd and to drive them to this place she came from would be no small undertaking.

"A dozen would not be enough?" he asked.

She looked back at him from tending the baby on the other cot. "No, me need big herd."

"You have some horses to ride?"

"Two."

He winced moving his sore shoulder, and his left arm hurt to the core. Be a day or two before he could use it. How many bands of wild ones were loose in the country? Must be several close by for "Wayne" to have set up camp at this place. He and she had been there since the summer before—took nine months to make a baby. Must have been a real loner, to chase bangtails by himself. Somewhere there would be some letters or papers in that trunk to tell Slocum more about her dead man.

"Can I look in the trunk?" He looked over at her.

She gave him an affirmative nod, and he went to the camelback, opened the lid and saw some woolen underwear, a pair of new waist overalls, two collarless shirts, a six-gun wrapped in a holster. Then neatly tied in a bundle were some well-worn letters.

Wayne Coats, General Delivery. Billings, Montana. Slocum opened the envelope and let the letter unfold.

> *Dear Wayne,*
>
> *Your dear wife Sarie ain't well. She are staying at grandpaws and cant live much longer—the consumption got her so bad. I never tole her I write you, cause you breaked her heart leaving. Your boy Norman run off with a circus, we thank. Been gone fur months now. You git this—send me money to put away Sarie. Your daughter Desera is ah living in sin down on Coon Crick with Averal Thomas. I threat to kill him but I decide then I be just like you and be on the run if'n I did kills him.*
>
> *Things ain't good here—send me money for the funeral. Them law don't ask much anymore about you. Ain't no excuse to come back.*
> *Your brother, Morgan*

"What it say?"

"His name's Wayne Coats. He was wanted by the law in—" He turned the letter over and read the faded cancellation. Rolla, Missouri. Two years earlier.

The second letter was in a very fancy script. The address Fort Lincoln, Dakota Territory.

My darling Wayne,

You have been gone from Joplin for six months. The reward poster is still up in the sheriff's office. However, I have found myself in a very difficult position. Your child has my stomach swollen so large I seldom go out in public. I realize that you no doubt have your wife and two children back in Rolla to provide for, but I will have several bills with the delivery of the child that are more than my modest income can sustain.

So at your earliest convenience please send me two hundred dollars, so I may travel to St. Charles and birth it in a secluded place. That way it will be born in a church facility there and they will place it in a good Christian home.

I know now how foolish we were not to think of this happening, but when you consider my deepest love for you, you will come to my rescue. So please send the money post haste.
Your love forever,
Charlene Severs

Slocum shook his head.
The other letters were forwarded from Billings to Idaho Falls, Idaho, and Charlene pleaded in each for his financial help. The last one was from St Charles, Missouri.

Dear Wayne,

I hope this letter finds you in good health. The child was stillborn and is interned in the churchyard. I have met a man here, recently widowed, and I will become his bride in a few weeks. He has three small children and they are well mannered. So this letter will sever our connection. I do not do this lightly. I have looked for you to return to me in my days of discomfort and need. But alas you never came.

You must know about the death of your poor wife, Sarie. Our cousin Myra wrote me from Rolla that she passed away last month. Oh, I saw your son on the streets of St. Charles. He was riding with some dis-

*respectful men, outlaws I suspect. He did not recognize
me I am certain.*

*I hope you are safe and alive. Why you never an-
swered my small requests for the necessary money I
shall never know. But Edgar is so generously taking
over my debts and we shall have a good life together.
I hope you find happiness too.*
Good-bye forever,
your cousin Charlene

"What in them?" she asked.

"Sad women."

"No understand."

"He had many wives, besides you."

She narrowed her thick lashes and peered at him hard.
"Him Mormon?"

"No, just had lots of wives."

"They want him back?"

"No. I think they all wanted you to have him." Then he
laughed and she laughed, too.

His strength returned slower than he liked. To occupy his
mind, he repaired Wayne's saddle lacings. The use of his left
arm began to build, and they rode to inspect several brush
corrals that Wayne built. Slocum was impressed by his
craftsmanship. The pens were stout, and it was obvious that
the man had known lots about wild horses. His traps were
not obvious until the animal was through the gates and it was
too late to turn around.

"You help him build these?"

She nodded. "Never let me chase them."

"Why not?"

"Him go alone."

"After the mustangs?" He saw her nod and wondered
about the man who raped an Indian girl, made her his wife
and called her "Squaw." He must have been a real nice guy
from what Slocum had read in the letters, too.

He searched the clear blue sky and prepared to mount up.
"Tomorrow, we begin moving horses."

She smiled big at him. "Be good time."

"Tell me something." He dropped to his heels to squat close to her while she fed more brush to the cooking fire.

"Was he here to help you when the baby was born?"

"No. After I bury him, a few days, Wine come."

"No one helped you have the baby?"

She shook her head and looked at him as if to say *Can't you understand? I was all alone.*

He put his hand on her shoulder and shook his head in sympathy. "You are a strong person, Squaw." Calling her that was hard; he wished she had a name. Oh well, that was what she was used to. He looked off toward the low hills. Must have been something, delivering your own child out there with only the damn coyotes for help. A shiver ran up his spine at the thought of the birthing happening and her all alone. Cold chills popped out on the back of his arms under Wayne's shirt she'd given him to wear.

Dawn spread light across the land. In the coolness, he finished cinching the saddle and led the dun she called Bob out of the trap. He put back the bars. This was the stout Texas cow pony Wayne had been riding when she said he was killed. An accident on a steep hillside and not the horse's fault.

She pointed to the northeast. "Plenty mustangs up there."

"Good. You and Little Wayne rest today. Let me find them."

"Plenty of them up there." She acted disappointed he was leaving her there. She chewed on her lower lip, uncertain looking.

"I'll find them. Be back."

She rushed over and put her hand on his leg. "You be careful."

Her words made him nod and smile. Holding the papoose in her other arm, the wind flapping the small blanket he was wrapped in, she stood straight backed and proud. "We get plenty horses."

"We will," he promised her and rode out.

Mid-morning, he found a dozen outcasts. Two- and three-year-olds, awkward males driven from the herd by the main stallion and living at enough distance from the mares to stay out of the way of the herd boss' wrath. Each was a stud intended to kill any male past a yearling that ever tried to breed one of his mares or usurp his rule of the band and privilege to be the only server.

This gangly bunch threw up their heads and moved away at Slocum's approach. Since they had not been chased in some time, he hoped that they would not spook too much if he fell in behind them. The nearest pen she had shown him was several miles to the south. So being as easy as he could, he rode after the ten head in a long trot once he had them moving in the right direction.

They dropped into a wide, grassy coulee and tried to turn back to the east. But he rode out on a point, and the sight of him made them toss their unkempt manes and go back to where they came off the bank.

Soon they were headed southward again and he fell in on their backtrail. A couple of red roans with black manes and tails, four bays, a bald-faced one that looked sharp to him, a strawberry roan with a light mane and tail, a sorrel and two calico paints made up the band. Trotting along, they showed their teeth at each other in the typical peck order fashion of all pack animals. One was the boss hoss, and Slocum decided the bald-faced one was the number one. Everyone cowered back a little from him.

Not always in the lead, the bald-faced one still held command. The ponies showed little herd pattern, acting more like a loose confederation than a band—nonetheless, Baldy was the aloft one, and with a show of teeth and sideways kick for effect, he put any challenger in the bunch on the run.

By noon, with the range of hills growing closer, the mustangs acted more and more like they wanted to turn back north. Obviously their basic instinct was to be near the mares, in case they ever got a chance to breed one. But only in the case that the stallion became lame, sick or died did such juveniles ever luck out. Still, procreation was implanted so deep in their male minds that it led them even to their own deaths at the hooves and teeth of the stud, for a single chance to have sex.

Mid-afternoon, Slocum had made several runs right and left thwarting their efforts to break back. Each time, seeing him, they tossed their heads and, reluctant acting, trotted southward. Their hooves turned up dust, and the wind swept it from them, though their backs were floured and their shoulders were now dark with sweat. The ponies probably wanted a drink as bad as he did.

Slocum could see the gap in the hills where Wayne's eastmost trap was concealed, a deep slice in the wall-like row of hills. An obvious game trail led into it, and the fenced-in spring up there made it ideal. Despite Wayne's strange ways, his mind must have possessed a keen sense of animal ways, Slocum decided as he loped up the steep slope to catch sight of the horses.

More worried about them veering right or left on the wide bench, he sent Bob uphill in hard cat hops. The horses were stopped, eyeing him warily as a group. Acting undecided about his threat, they tossed their heads at his approach and went on. Their action drew a small smile on Slocum's face. His shoulder had begun to throb and he felt light-headed from going most of the day without water or food. Still, he was close to finishing the easiest drive he figured there would be.

Single file, they headed up the narrow confine. He could see horses considering the almost sheer slopes on either side. A desperate horse might make it up that, so Slocum undid the lariat and put spurs to Bob with a loud scream to dissuade them from any idea of escaping.

Don't leave anything to chance. Time to force them into a panic, before they even considered the alternative way to go. Tails sucked to their butts, the youngsters fled in pandemonium. Half-jumping over each other, they filed up the canyon until Slocum slid to a halt and dismounted to move the panels of poles lashed to posts that Wayne had obviously spent hours building. Setting up the stout sections made his wound ache and head pound. But nothing was going to spoil his crowning moment of closure. The ten head standing in a row eyed him with curiosity from the confines.

"And only forty more to go," he said and loosened the cinch on Bob.

He swept off Wayne's felt hat she had given him and wiped his face on the sleeve of the man's shirt, another gift. Then with a look off to the sky, he nodded to his long gone donor. Mighty fine of him to leave so much.

Be long past dark when he got back to camp. The mustangs would find the tank of water. They didn't need anything else until he returned. He hated to tell them, but he planned some grim things ahead for the ten of them. It would all take time. He hoped he found the energy for the task— at the moment, he felt done in enough to drop on the dirt and sleep away the rest of his life.

At last, he tightened his latigos and climbed on Bob. With a nod of his head, he set out in a long trot for camp and her. There would be an evening meal waiting—rabbit stew or grouse browned on a spit over a fire—and she would be standing on a high point concerned, watching for him, thinking he might have ridden away and left her forever. Perhaps even doubting he would ever return.

Calling her Squaw would never do, he decided on the ride back. He'd need to rename her. He could hear the plaintive whinny of the confused colts in the trap behind him when he dropped down the steep slope. He'd be back, they had no need to fear.

The sun had long set behind the far-off snowcap of Mount Rainier when he came up beside Crab Creek on a slow lope. Coyotes were yapping at the rising quarter moon. And a hoot owl swung in an arcing circle overhead as if checking him out.

He reined up and saw her jump up from the fire.

"You plenty late," she said, coming over in a flurry of leather fringe.

"How many mustangs did I get?" he asked, dismounting and then undoing the latigos one-handed to save his sore shoulder.

"You got some? How many?"

He held up ten fingers and she drew her head back in dismay. "So many?"

The next thing he knew she tackled him, then went to hugging him, and singing some Indian song he didn't recognize, but it sounded victorious. Despite the sharp pain in his shoulder she caused him, he smiled down into her face when she looked up at him pleased with the news.

He raised her chin up higher on the side of his hand and kissed her mouth. She blinked in shock.

"What that?"

He could see her look at him questioning his action as well. "Kiss. You've never been kissed?"

She straightened and stood on her toes. "Me like."

Despite the complaint in his shoulder, he took her in his arms and kissed her this time for real. When he finished, he looked down into her dreamy eyes.

"Better eat . . ." she managed. Then she slipped like an otter out of his arms and went to get him some food.

He took a place on the small, twisted log dragged up for a seat and listened to the night sounds. When she handed him his plate, he nodded in approval.

"What color are they?" she asked, sitting beside him, anxious for a description of his catch.

"You will have to see them."

"Are they pretty?"

He nodded between bites.

"No coffee," she apologized. "Tea?"

"Yes. You may have to go to town and buy some coffee." She never answered.

"You afraid to go to town?" He glanced over at her, anxious to taste the spoonful of her stew.

"You say—me go."

"After we get these horses gentled."

She nodded, then bent over and put her forehead on his sore shoulder. "Ten horses, one day—oh, you make good man." Her finger clutched his arm and he winced.

"Slocum."

"Slo-cum," she repeated.

4

After he finished eating and she fed the baby, she came and sat beside him on the ground. The sharp smell of the small sagebrush fire filled his nose, and the soft light of the small red flames danced on her face. He smoked a small pipe from Wayne's things. Despite the dryness of the old tobacco, the nicotine relaxed him and he savored each puff.

A million stars pricked the vast dark canopy overhead. Slocum felt the stiffness of his shoulder when he flexed it, but her willow bark tea had already begun to ease much of the pain. There had been no sign of anyone in days. She, the baby, he, a dozen coyotes and some magpies were the sum total population of the valley, besides the mustang herds. Several of them—he'd heard stallions challenge each other and saw in the distance several sizeable bands. Off in the night, a coyote yipped and another answered.

"Where do you go?" she asked.

"Like a dust devil, where the wind takes me."

"You have no people?"

"None." He lied. He had a brother, but no idea where he was or if he was still alive. All that brought back sad memories. Spanish moss in the oak trees. Alabama and the deep woods with oaks and chestnuts so big around three men could not span them holding hands. Funny how in a land of a few scraggly cottonwoods, he would think about such things. Fields of cotton and corn, sluggish streams of water full of fish.

"Do you have a family?" he asked.

She nodded.

"Miss them?"

"It would be nice to be with them." She scratched with a small twig in the hard dirt before her.

"When we catch the horses, will you go back?"

"Long ways." She raised up and looked out into the night. The coyotes were yapping again in the west.

"We better get some sleep. Those horses will mean lots of work tomorrow," he said.

She agreed and stretched her arms over her head. "Cayuse God send you to me."

"No, the lady of fate sent me here. And I'm grateful."

"Who?"

He raised his hand to wave off any concern. "It is only a saying."

"You know a woman with a baby should not *nicky-do,*" she said, her face a mask of concern as she looked at him for his answer.

"Nicky—do?"

"Lay with her man," she said quickly and turned away like she dared not look at him any longer.

"Oh."

Then in the faint light he saw her gaze turn toward him. "You get in plenty bad way, we *nicky-do.*"

He leaned toward her and kissed her mouth. The back of her hand flew to her lips like he had burned them. When he drew back, her eyes turned to dark saucers.

"White men do strange things to their women," she said, from behind her hand.

"Some do, some don't." He rose to his feet. Better quit for one night or he'd have to *nicky-do* her or whatever she called it.

"Tomorrow, we need to start on the horses. You have a brand?"

She drew a deep breath, then nodded. On her feet, she

disappeared around the tent and returned with two irons.
They were a bar and a W.

"How do they go?"

She pointed to the bar first, then the W.

"Good. Let's get some sleep."

"Slo-cum—you good man for me."

"We'll see," he said and followed her inside the tent.

On the cot, gazing at the dark canvas roof, he considered the
three tasks: rope break the horses, brand and geld them—not
necessarily in that order. He fell half-asleep recalling all he
could about the last process. In his youth, a man came around
each year to handle the surgery of making neuters out of
studs. Best he could recall, the operation could be unsuccessful if done improperly, and the animal, though sterile,
would still have the characteristics and desire of a full male.
They called them proud cut. Hours later, he found some
sleep.

Sounds of her cooking outside woke him. He threw his
legs over the side of the cot, sat up in his underwear and
rubbed his sleepy face in his calloused palms. Still before
dawn, it was dark in the tent. He pulled on his pants and put
up the galluses. Next his socks and boots. He'd put on his
shirt later. More important at the moment, he went out back
to empty his bladder.

"Morning."

She looked up and nodded at him as he went off a few
yards. With his back to her, the fresh sage smell on the cool
air sweeping his face, he undid his fly, uncurled his manhood
and soon let loose. The bladder pressure abating, he savored
the relief and closed his eyes, still half-asleep. As he stood
there arcing his pee off into the dry earth and bunchgrass,
he about laughed out loud over her word for sex—*nicky-do*.

He'd have to remember that word if he ever found another
Cayuse woman. Oriental women called it *poon-tang*. He re-
called escorting a wagon load of them from Cheyenne to
Deadwood. All of them talking at once sounded like geese.
And anything set them off with a sharp "Oh!"

He'd been to the side, thinking he was unobserved and

pissing like that, when three of them Oriental sisters must have been spying on him, saw it, and they did the same thing—exclaimed aloud at their discovery. For all he could learn from them, Chinese men were not so well endowed— though he never made any crotch inspection of the Eastern male population, the slant-eyed maidens acted like his was a big prize. During that week-long drive to the Black Hills, he tried not to disappoint any of them.

Whenever the chance came and he was aside from the others, one would make jerky steps in her platform shoes to catch him, saying, "You wait. You wait."

When he stopped, she would smile and nod at him as if to ask, *You weady foo me?*

The coast was clear. Out of sight in some draw or behind a stand of junipers, he would nod at her. She would bend over, throw the long skirt over her back and present the two halves of her small butt to him. Must have been how the sailors taught them to do it on the boat they came over on.

There she was bent over, smiling back and waiting patiently while he built an erection looking down at her skinny ass. When he stepped up close behind her, her small hand reached out, grasped his tool and inserted it in her slick cunt. By then his hips ached to probe her, and with her small waist in both hands he began to give her what for. Soon they were both huffing like train engines, and he slid his right hand in under her flat belly and into her seam. A Chinese woman has little hair down there compared to a white women or even Indians. When his finger found the rock-hard ridge of his plunging dick, he traced back until he found the knob above it to rub with his fingertip.

"Oh!" she cried in a shrill voice, and from there on she moaned and groaned in deep Chinese pleasure, a separate sound from any other race of woman he ever had sex with.

The walls of her pussy began to swell and he worked harder, slamming his dick into her until he finally came and she wilted. Many times, they fainted on him at that point, and he was forced to withdraw and hold them by the waist in his arms until they recovered.

These girls were a surplus commodity in their own land.

Daughters of poor farmers in the back provinces, they were sold into slavery, loaded aboard leaking vessels and trained in their trade by horny sailors on the long voyage to the States. With new clothes to wear, enough food to eat each day, they showed few qualms about their newfound vocation; in fact, they acted like they enjoyed it—especially with him.

Of course, the man in charge, Lou Fagan, earned a huge fortune on his investment of three hundred dollars per head that he made in San Francisco, where immigration officials looked aside at their entry for a fee. In Deadwood, under the tutelage of Molly Cosby, a madam of cow town fame, they turned lots of tricks for piles of gold dust. Fagan also sold individual girls to the Chinese men for the flat sum of ten thousand in gold for a wife—a shorter commodity in the new world. Fagan did a rather brisk business according to reports, until an angry loser in a poker game stuck a stiletto under his ribs and killed him.

Later, after his demise, Slocum heard how Molly sold the rest of the girls to the highest bidders, bought a wooden marker for Fagan's grave, which was over on the hill with Wild Bill and Calamity Jane's, that read,

Here lies Lou Fagan
Knifed to death
He won't ever fuck again
Nor take a breath

The head board was removed two years later by a group of temperance women. Meanwhile, the robust, buxom Molly bought a huge house in Denver, and being rich as anyone, she lived the life of a society woman, even married the former city mayor Harlan Doone.

Slocum drew another deep breath of the sagey air, put his dick away and buttoned his pants, still thinking about those slant-eyed sisters' small butts as he went back to her fire. He squatted down and she poured him some tea.

"When you say, I will go to town." Her dark serious eyes met his.

He nodded as she bent over and spooned him out some

thick oatmeal into a bowl. Without sweetener, the hot cereal was not that inviting to him, but it would keep him from being hungry before evening. He suspected his next meal would be long after sundown.

"The baby will be all right going along over there?" he asked, seated on the ground, eating his spoons of oats slow-like.

"Fine," she said and came to sit by him. "Him can learn about mustanging from his papoose."

"How much tea is left?" He meant the hard-pressed bars from the orient that she shaved to make their tea.

"One or two."

He nodded that he heard her. How much money did he have? Perhaps less than ten dollars. His luck at cards the last night in town had been minimal. But that much would buy enough supplies to last them for a while. He flexed his left shoulder—not all the way healed, but it would be okay.

"Wayne have much money," she said.

"How much?"

She smiled, set aside her bowl and went for the tent. In a few seconds, she returned with a new-looking canvas sack and handed it to him. The weight shocked him. He reached inside and came out with a few crisp discs. Turned to the fire's light, he looked hard at the freshly minted twenty-dollar gold pieces. Why, there must be a fortune in the bag.

How did a mustanger get such a sack of money? There could be as much as a thousand dollars in the bag. Did she know the value?

"Where did he get it?" he asked her.

"Rob a train?" She looked in question at him.

"He did?"

She shook her head. "He say he found a train robber dead in coulee."

"Around here?"

She shook her head. "Idaho—he talk about it. Think I can't understand. Him ride up and see man on ground in coulee by his horse. Maybe him wounded. Wayne shoot him. Take money and him horse. Sell horse." She nodded her head. "Him talk plenty about it."

All kinds of secrets coming out about Wayne. He must have been a dandy to have left his wife and children, then took up with his own cousin and left her. Found a wounded train robber, shot and robbed him. Slocum shook his head in amazement—she had enough money to do whatever she wanted to do.

"Hide it," he said and she nodded.

Damn, men like those bounty hunters would have killed her in a second for that much money. Lucky no one ever knew, or there'd have been hell to pay. He was still upset by the money when they set out for the horse trap.

The sun was up when they reached the pen. The captives threw up their heads to look at them, still acting confused by their confinement and the future.

The future meant this strange creature on two legs throwing a snake at them. It encircled one's neck and soon the restraint was wrapped on a post and in head-shaking fashion the horse fought the rope until choked down, then Slocum loosened it and made a halter. He forefooted the horse, laid him on the ground and bound his feet, and she brought the hot iron. A smell of burned hair soon filled Slocum's nose, and he nodded to her at the sight of the fresh brown markings—a bar and a W with blackened hair around it.

Slocum removed his jackknife, which he'd sharpened on a stone enroute. The horse, on his side, raised his head to protest, but by then his exposed scrotum was sliced open on both sides. The seeds removed, she ran back with a hot iron to sear the end of the severed cord to stop any excess bleeding. Slocum wore a thick glove to protect his hand. The task complete, he motioned for her to step aside as she took both fist-sized gonads in her hands to save for their supper. Reaching over the horse, to be out of range of any kick, Slocum undid the tie. Moving quickly, he grasped ahold of the youngster's tail and forced the shaky-legged colt to his feet.

Wobbly, the gelding dragged the lead rope and staggered away.

"That's one," Slocum said.

She nodded in grim approval.

"He was an easy one." He wiped his sweaty face on the dirty sleeve.

"Get you drink," she said and ran off to get him water from the spring.

Soon the catching and surgery was repeated until, by the time the sun hung low in the west, the last colt was neutered and dragging a rope. The mustangs looked downcast standing about straddle legged, but the toughest part was over. The rest would be much easier on them.

Slocum went to the spring and washed his face and hands. She was seated in the long shade from the hill nursing her baby, looking equally done in. They still needed to get back to camp, over an hour's ride away. He went over and squatted on his heels beside her.

Behind her dust-floured face, she smiled at him, holding the baby to her breast. "Good job. You work hard today."

"Yes. We better get back to camp."

"Damn, you work plenty hard, Slo-cum."

"We both did."

She struggled to her feet. He rose, reached out and helped her. They exchanged a private look before he let go of her arm. Satisfied she was up, he set out for their mounts.

They rode back, with her talking about their supper of mountain oysters. He felt hungry enough to eat all of them as they rode in the twilight. When they dropped over the last ridge and he could see the cottonwoods, something struck him as being wrong—smoke coming from their camp. He held out his hand to stop her.

"You expecting company?"

She shook her head.

"Wait here and I'll check it out."

"Be careful," she said.

He nodded that he'd heard her and booted Bob forward. He undid the rawhide latch on his Colt hammer. Who the hell was stoking a fire up in their camp? Bounty hunter? The law? He'd learn soon enough.

Then he saw them stand up, three forms wrapped in blankets in the firelight—Injuns. Were they her kin? He reined up Bob and let her catch up. Damn, what did this mean?

She led the way into camp after he explained to her who was there. From the glare in her eyes, she did not seem over-joyed by their appearance. In the pearly starlight, he could see the confusion on her face at his words. At last, she shook her head. "Me go see."

His hand on the butt of his Colt, he rode behind her. Not likely they'd cut down a woman, especially a squaw. The three stood back from the fire when they rode into camp.

"Ho!" she shouted and they nodded. Slocum slipped off Bob as she remained mounted, talking in guttural language to the men. They acted disinterested in her, but their dark eyes followed Slocum.

He moved closer to her. What did those three want any-way? The tall one answered her—straight-backed, he acted like some aloft chief. And went to talking Cayuse, Slocum figured, like he was giving her orders.

"Who are they?" he asked in a stage whisper.

"Running Dog, big one."

"Who's he?"

"He comes to ask for me to be his wife."

He scowled at her. "Who are the others?"

"Short one is Tall Horse. Boy is calling Laughing Deer."

"Why did they come here?" Slocum frowned at the whole business—he didn't like how the tall one talked to her.

"Dog need wife."

"He have one?"

She held up three fingers.

"Three, hell, why does he need you?" He kept a sharp eye on them, not trusting they wouldn't try something.

"One wife is sick, one is big with baby, other one is lazy."

"You going with him?"

"No." She shook her head vehemently.

"Good. What now?"

"Feed them."

"Yes. We have enough to go around," he agreed, thinking about all the gonads, though he still did not like the way the big bucks looked at either of them. He obviously came to get another wife, not to be turned down.

She must have told them she would cook for them. The three quickly sat on the ground, too much like they were determined to stay awhile and hope she changed her mind about becoming the tall one's fourth wife.

Slocum took the horses off to hobble and let them graze. Why did he feel so wary of those bucks? Something kept nudging him about the threesome—oh well, he'd have to see how it turned out. Been better if they'd rode on when she said no.

Then the coyotes yapping off in the sage distracted him. Well, they didn't act too warlike for Injuns.

When he came back, she was roasting the fist-size oysters over her fire. He squatted down beside her.

"What made him come here? Because Wayne was dead?" he asked softly.

"Maybe. Make him think I leave you."

"What did you tell him?"

"I your woman now."

"What did he say to that?" Slocum scowled at the three of them, then turned back.

"'He is a white man. Why you put up with him?'"

"Good question," he said, pouring himself some tea from her pot into his tin cup.

"They would never have hobbled the horses. That woman's work. They think you are—" She quit and shook her head.

"That I'm a sissy for doing that?"

"Sissy?"

"Not a warrior?"

She nodded quickly, then turned the sizzling meat. He rose with his cup and went to where the three sat under their blankets on the log. The flames of her fire made wavering red light on their solemn, dark faces.

"After you eat, you leave, Running Dog," he said. "This is my camp. She's my woman."

The long-faced buck's eyes narrowed and he threw out his chest. "We three, you one."

"Why let two dumb boys die and you still have to leave afterwards?"

"How you kill them?"

"I would shoot them in the eye and you in the guts, so you could think about it while you died in pain."

"You talk tough for white man."

"I am tough, Running Dog. Don't try me. You have insulted my woman and me by so boldly coming here asking for her to leave me." He sipped his tea looking hard over the rim. Then, meeting the buck's hard stare, he dropped the cup, his hand flew to his hip, and the Colt cleared leather and cocked in the same lithe move. None of the three moved, but they looked uncomfortable facing the revolver's bore.

"We leave," Running Dog said.

The other two looked relieved when Slocum dropped the muzzle and spun the cylinder so the hammer fell on an empty. Holstered, he swept up the cup. "Better come eat. She has it ready."

They ate their supper on that side of the fire. He joined her on the opposite side.

"What you tell them?"

"Eat and leave. That you were my woman and this was my camp." He took a seat cross-legged and then accepted the tin plate of roasted oysters from her. If those three were armed, it was an old rifle concealed under their blanket.

"You good man, Slocum." She nodded her head in solemn approval.

"Sometimes," he told her, not missing much the three-some did as they devoured her cooking. Finished, Running Dog stood up and walked to the fire.

"Nomie, your man says this his camp and we must leave." She rose and nodded in agreement.

"A Cayuse would never turn away men in the dark night."

"No, a Cayuse kill you for asking him wife to leave him."

"Your white eyes never know if you not tell him."

Her spine stiffened. "I not unfaithful."

"When he leaves you, you come back to the reservation like bitch with tail between your legs."

"When I come back I be a rich woman with many horses and choose own man."

Running Dog shook his head in disbelief. "He have it all

then and leave you for white woman. You have nothing but him ugly breed children to raise."

"Go!" Slocum shouted, having heard enough of his words in English to be insulted by them. He set the plate of food aside and rose to his feet. Enough was enough.

The three left in the night. He stood for a long while considering their disappearance. They weren't gone. They'd try something—maybe even an attempt on his life. Did they know about the horses in the trap? He expected some mischief in camp from them. The matter wasn't over between them yet.

"Will they come back?" he asked her.

She nodded, looking grave. "You should have killed them."

"I thought that right off when you told me their intentions." Ruefully, he shook his head. He should have shot them then and told God they died. Damn, his qualms about murdering them outright would cost him before it was all over.

5

Seated cross-legged on the rise, the .44–40 lever-action across his lap, Slocum awaited the sun's first crest in the east. A cool breeze swept his face. Out in the sage, a grouse called to his mate. Other birds began to stir. Ravens had taken wing. A late-returning coyote trotted by the edge of camp, sniffing the air as if to find something to eat, his nocturnal hunt obviously unsuccessful for he acted bolder than most of his kind. Then as if he had drawn a fearful scent, he sucked his tail to his butt and bolted away.

Slocum cocked the hammer back on the Winchester, above the gurgle of the creek. The weariness of spending the night on guard was swept away, replaced by a fresh, new alertness. Every muscle in his body tensed in readiness, the cramps in his legs gone, the stiffness in his shoulders no longer binding him. He swept the area across the stream for any sign of them.

He heard a strange horse cough. Not from one of their two who were grazing to his right. He noticed Bob, who had raised his head looking to the south. The other pony did the same. Slocum dropped down on his stomach, convinced the horses knew more than he did about the surprise attack. Then he spotted the youngest buck in a flash of brown. Stripped down to a loincloth, with a bow and arrow in his hand, he came in a bent-over trot out of the right-hand draw. No cover for him if he started for the camp—Slocum could drop him anytime.

Where were the others? On foot or horseback? Then he spotted the head of a single horse. Cruel to shoot a horse, but his action might save him from having to eventually shoot the three of them. All he wanted was them gone— damn stupid bucks. She'd already told them no.

He tried to consider how they would come—who would be the last one. Then he glanced back at the tent. There was struggle inside, and soon, to his dismay, he saw Tall Horse appear holding a knife to her throat.

"Kill them!" she shouted in defiance, still struggling with the buck.

Slocum rose with the rifle in his hands. Damn. They'd managed to outmaneuver him. He allowed the gun to drop. Deer came tearing over and jerked the .44 out of his holster and grinned, looking at the well-oiled weapon. He motioned for Slocum to head for the tent. Filled with disgust, Slocum obeyed, wondering what would happened next.

He was not prepared for Tall Horse to rush outside of the tent and strip the baby from the papoose. Squaw's wailing didn't affect the brutal act. Horse took the child by the heels and smashed his small head on the log. Not once, but three times he swung the infant over his head and down hard, until the child's skull was a bloody mess. Squaw fought hard to get to him, and it took all of Dog's strength to contain her. At last, Dog hit her over the head and her knees buckled. She was sprawled on the ground at his feet as Dog and Horse had a verbal contest about who could holler the loudest.

Dog ordered the boy, Deer, to get the things out of the tent. He sent the sullen Horse to get their ponies and turned his attention to Slocum. "I would kill you, but then the soldiers would come for us. Your lucky day, huh?"

"I can count the ones you have left to live," Slocum said, still shaken by the Indian's brutal murder of the baby. But he thought he saw their reason. They were taking her back with them, so with the breed child dead, she had no reason to deny them sex. Plus he was an unpure and they had no place in either the red or white world for them. Still he shook his head and shuddered at their callousness.

Dog tried to lift her by the arm. "Wake up, ugly squaw. Fix food."

At last, she responded. Groggy, she fought her way to her feet and staggered off to obey him.

"You go sit on the ground here." He ordered Slocum to move closer to her cooking fire, so he could watch both of them.

Horse brought in Bob and the bay to pile the stuff on them they intended to take along. Deer tossed Wayne's saddle on Bob, then began hanging on his back sacks and things taken from the tent.

"Under the log," she whispered. "Money."

Under scrutiny of the threesome, Slocum dared to wink at her to show he heard her as she labored with her kettles hanging over the fire. He'd have money if he needed some to recover her. How and in what shape they'd leave him, besides afoot, were the next questions. The money was hidden under the log, where Horse had tossed the limp body of her child. Any revenge was too good for the likes of these three. Slocum regretted not shooting them and asking questions later the first time they were in their camp, but no, he'd had to be fair. Fuck being fair.

The three ate, giving him hard looks and obviously making plans in their own lingo. Whatever plans they made would not be good for him or her. No sense him trying anything—they had the weapons, save for the .30-cal fist-size handgun concealed in his boot top. It would be needed before this was over.

At last, they bound his hands and legs. Leaving him trussed up, Dog forced her to get on his horse and left with both saddle horses loaded down with all but the tent, cots and trunk.

"Don't follow us," Dog warned. "We will kill you if you do."

Slocum never said a word, sitting in the growing daylight, just listened to them ride away. They wanted out of this country as quick as possible. Whether they feared the Army or other whites, he wasn't certain, but they had left fast. As soon as he figured they were out of hearing, he began to roll for the creek. The effort hurt his shoulder. They'd tied him with leather, and in water it stretched. In minutes, he was half-soaked, but the ties came loose around his wrist and he soon tore at the binds on his leg.

Flexing his fingers and rubbing them to get the circulation going, he began to lay his plans. His pursuit of them would not be as quick as he desired, but that might convince them he wasn't coming after her at all. The .30-caliber in his waistband, he struggled to his feet. He needed next to go pick out a colt to ride. He looked to the sky. They were over an hour away, maybe longer on foot.

He went to the log and rolled it over. The loose dirt was obvious in the morning light. Searching around, he found the small spade somehow overlooked by the pilferers. He dug up the money sack and laid it aside. Using a piece of blanket, he rolled the small, stiff body of Little Wayne in it and placed the bundle in the hole. After covering it with dirt, he rolled the log back over it to protect the child's remains from varmints digging them up. Then, with her money pouch stuffed in his shirt, a rope they missed coiled over his shoulder and some sacks in a bundle, he headed for the faraway pen of young horses.

He judged it close to midday when he finally watered at the spring and drew the anxious snorts of the colts in the pen.

He roped the bald-faced horse, snubbed him to a post and beat him with the sacks until the colt no longer spooked. He named him Baldy in the process. Then he fashioned a jaw bridle and swung on his back. Standing straddle legged, the colt did nothing. Slocum jerked the horse's head back, but the next jumps were halfhearted. Then Slocum booted him with his heels and he hit a stiff buck. When the bucking didn't work, the horse began to run to escape the one on his back. But he soon discovered that, too, would not work and set into a long, swinging walk.

Slocum knew Baldy was stiff from the previous day's surgery—the only advantage he had. Fresh as he acted, he'd have been hard to top off that easy without the trauma of the past day to knock some of the wild energy out of him. Slocum slid off at the gate and threw it open to let the rest out, too. Then in a bound he was on his pony and headed west. He almost laughed at the strange look the others gave him before he rode off.

He bet they wondered what was going on. Looking for an Injun girl needed his attention. On the long bench of the mountainside, he rode west to cut her abductors' tracks. Some places he had to skirt deep draws, but basically the tableland held, and he rode through the sage and tall grasses, disturbing a few grouse, jackrabbits and other birds. He finally cut the Injuns' trail going over the mountain in mid-afternoon. By suppertime, he had crossed over the top and could see the great horseshoe bend of the Columbia beneath him.

Good enough—somewhere down there would be someone who had a horse and saddle to sell. He dismounted and started down the steepest part leading his reluctant steed. When the grade grew less, he bounded onto the horse's back and rode again. No sign of anyone below, but he was a long ways from the river, and below was desert as well.

Close to sundown, following the river's course, he spotted some smoke and turned Baldy in the direction of it. When he topped a rise, he saw the efforts of someone's clearing the sage, and some corrals, rough buildings and a shack in the hillside where the smoke came from a stovepipe.

"Hello the house!" he shouted, leading the less-than-trained Baldy by the jaw rope.

"Hello." She stood in the doorway in a blue checkered dress, a woman in her early twenties, with a willowy figure and pleasant-looking oval face. Her reddish brown hair shone in waves to her shirt collar.

"I need to buy a horse," he said and fashioned a halter out of the rope to tie up Baldy unless she ran him off.

"Well, I can't help you, stranger. I have none." She indicated the corral, which was empty. "Howard has the team. He's gone to town to try and hire some help."

"Yes, ma'am." He swept off his hat, with Baldy tied securely to a post. "Well, could I buy some lunch?"

"No."

"Well, thanks anyway." He started to undo the rope.

"Wait! What I meant to say was you can't buy any. Not you can't have any."

"Yes, ma'am."

"Well, I'll get some water and you can wash up," she said.

"Name's Slocum," he said after her.

"Kathren," she said and disappeared.

He scrubbed his hands and whisker-stubbled face at the table beside the door. Then he dried himself on a flour-sack towel. When he finished, she nodded in approval and invited him inside.

The room consisted of a bed under a fine quilt, a table, two chairs, a dry sink and a fancy cooking range with chrome corners and an oven above and below. She motioned toward the table and chairs. In seconds, she had a bowl of stew set before him, yellow corn bread and fresh creamy butter set out and was pouring him coffee in a crock mug.

"There, that should do for starters."

"Do me fine, ma'am."

"Kathren."

"Yes," he said, with his first bite of her food drawing the saliva in his mouth.

"How long since you ate last?" she asked, taking a seat opposite him.

"Two days ago."

"I better heat up some more."

"This will be fine," he protested, lathering butter on a corn bread square. "You said your husband was looking for help."

"You need work?"

"No."

"Didn't figure you for the sagebrush-grubbing kind when I saw you. Howard's not my husband. My husband died in Idaho two years ago. See, Frank and Howard were partners. We came out here from back east. Ohio. Oh, Idaho was sure not the best place I've ever been." She dropped her gaze to her lap and shook her head. "First Howard's wife Marie ran off and left him."

"Left him in Idaho?"

"Went off to work in house—you know what I mean. Couldn't talk her out of it."

He paused between bites. "Had she ever—"

"Worked in one before? Oh, no. But she got so upset doing without things like having a house of her own and a roof over her head, and all the storms we went through getting there never helped. She said any house would be better than that damn wagon and him."

"Must've had her mind made up. Reckon she ever regretted it?"

"I don't think so." She shook her head. "My husband, Frank, died two days later. Busted appendix, they thought. So after that, Howard and I decided to go on. He couldn't stand to be in the same place with his wife working in the house, and I couldn't face looking at where Frank died."

"You two get married?"

She shook her head. "I don't think Howard could ever get married again. He really loved her, and well, I think she took part of him with her."

Slocum nodded. The food was beginning to fill him. He didn't need to get sick by overeating.

"I been looking at you," she said. Then her hand flew to her mouth and her face turned red. "I mean, your clothes need washing. Frank was about your size. They're too large for Howard. I could dress you in some better ones, if you wished."

"I don't want to be any trouble to you."

"You're no trouble. You're the third person beside Howard I've talked to this year." She dropped her chin and shook her head. "His poor wife would never have made it out here. She's best off back there."

"I imagine it does get lonely."

"Yes, and we have a cow to milk and chickens to feed, a fine sow expecting to farrow."

"So you stay close."

"Yes. Nearest post is two days by wagon, two days back."

Her blue eyes met his gaze. "You got time for a bath? My sheepherder's shower should be warm enough by now."

"Sun warms it?" he asked, familiar with such contraptions.

"Yes. Course, I'd have to refill it—"

"For you to take a shower?"

"Unless—"

"Well, maybe we could share that warm water."

Her blues eyes turned harder and she barely nodded. "You won't think bad of me?"

"No. Absolutely not."

"Good. You want me to shave you afterwards?"

"I'd like anything you want to do to me."

She stood up and extended her hand to him. "There's soap and towels down there."

He took her long hand and reeled her up to his chest. When his mouth closed on hers, she closed her eyes and he felt her go limp in his arms. Poor girl. She'd fainted. His arm behind her bent knees, he swept her up and smiled down at her as the long lashes fluttered. Without focus, the blue orbs blinked at him in disbelief.

"I never fainted before," she protested, as if in dreamland.

"No problem," he said and turned sideways to get his burden through the open doorway. Outside, he blinked in the bright sun and followed her head-toss directions to the sheepherder's shower.

"I think I can stand now," she said and he set her down.

He toed off his boots and watched her for any sign she might lose her balance. He grinned when she threw her head back to clear the dizziness away and began to undo the dress buttons down the front.

"Perhaps I'm not a brave as I thought."

He twisted away so she did not feel his eyes on her. There would be plenty of time to see her flesh later. No need to make her restless this early in the game.

"You have a wife?" she asked from behind him.

"No."

"Good."

He smiled to himself—her conscience must be sawing on

her. Over his shoulder, he said, "You can still back out."

"Back out—oh, no." Then she drew in her breath as if for courage. "I'm not afraid of you or—well, I know what I'm getting into. Do you?"

His pants unbuttoned, he removed them and strung them over the bench beside the slatted floor. He turned in time to see a pink nipple crowning the long pear-shaped globe exposed as she shrugged the dress off her shoulder.

"Yes," he said and stepped over to taste the honey on her lips. This time she answered his mouth, and her long fingers cupped the back of his head to hold him to her.

"Damn, it's been a long time," she said, out of breath. Out of her dress and her drawers, she raised up and pulled the rope.

Doused by the still not warmed water, she screamed and broke off laughing as she let go and the stream stopped. "I lied. It wasn't warm yet."

He attacked her with a bar of soap, running his lathered hands over her quaking, hard breasts, her back and firm derriere, until at last his hand cupped the coarse pubic hair and she closed her eyes in pleasure.

"My turn," she said and her fingers closed on his scrotum, then she explored his hardening shaft.

He began to wash the rest of himself, until she stepped in close and traced her rock-tight nipples over his chest. Satisfied he was clean enough, he pulled on the rope and the spout of cold water drenched them. Both free of soap, he scooped her up in his arms and headed for the open door of the shack.

Once inside, she begged for him to put her down. "I must save the quilt."

He set her on her bare feet, then watched her lithe form hurry over and turn back the colorful cover.

"Thanks. That is the only real treasure I have."

They met beside the rope bed and kissed. Their fall to the bed made the ropes squeak in protest. Hungry mouths sought each other in abandonment. Her sleek skin felt like a greased chute as they snuggled to be one. Her legs soon parted and he moved between them. Then with great effort, she raised her butt up off the sheet and his erection entered her gates.

Her openmouthed scream made goose bumps on the back of his arm. Then for reassurance and out of her need, she bear hugged him. Her nipples stabbed him like great nails in his chest. He sought for the depth of the tight shaft. His butt ached to pound her through the ropes.

Legs wrapped around his, she arched her back for more. Sweat ran down his face, and soon it lubricated their muscle-tight bellies as they worked in unison for the most pleasure. Harder and faster, until the skin on the head of his dick felt ready to burst.

"Ah!" she cried and went limp.

He felt her fluids rush out around his plug and down his scrotum. Her eyes swarmed in pools of blue, and weakly she smiled up at him.

"Don't quit," she whispered breathlessly.

In moments, she began to revive her strength, and he felt her begin to contract inside to his efforts. His head began to swirl with the pleasure of the moment, and her fingernails clawed at his butt, the edges biting into the hard flesh as he fought the war of passion.

He felt the explosion building deep in his testicles and jammed himself against her pubic bone for the blast that followed. Sharp pain from the opening stream made him drive in even deeper to escape the hurting. Two hot needles deep in his backside caused him to fire again inside her, and another volley followed that left him depleted in a wasted mass on top of her.

"Whew," she said as they untangled and came apart.

Sprawled on his back, he stared at the underside of the roof shingles. "Howard doesn't do that with you?"

She laughed aloud. "We've slept together in this bed for eighteen months. Not once has he even touched me."

"Maybe why his wife left him." He said his thoughts aloud.

"Perhaps—"

"Hey, it's none of my business."

"No, before I figured he was a man like Frank." Then she

raised up and grinned. "I was spoiled, I guess. My husband never had enough."

He pulled her face down and kissed her. Her palms slid over the ribbed muscles of his belly and soon found her goal. Slow like she began to pump it.

When she lifted her face up, she laughed. "You may be even better than he was at this."

"You ready for more?"

She fell over on her back and stared upward. "Maybe I should have gone with Marie. Yes, dammit, yes, because I know in an hour you're going to climb on that pony and leave me here. Aren't you?"

"Ever talk to him about your lives?"

"He says he ain't ready for another steady woman—yet."

"Well," he said, flexing the upper muscles of his back as he rolled over on top of her.

She put a finger to his mouth and scooted down for his entry. "Forget that dumb Howard."

Unable to contain his amusement, braced over the top of her, he looked down at her wonderful treasure chest and chuckled over her words. She shook her head in mock disapproval as she deftly reached under and stuck him back in her lubricated cunt. Then she snapped her eyes shut and acted ready for the pleasure to begin. Slocum closed his eyes in disbelief over his newfound situation and began to pump his way inside her.

Sorry, Squaw, but this *nicky-do* comes first—I'm coming, girl. Don't let them red devils hurt you.

6

She wouldn't take any money for the clothes she gave him or her husband's saddle. He strapped it on Baldy in the first light and prepared to climb aboard. She stood by the gate and threw her reddish hair back from her face. In the light, she hardly looked awake. He checked the bosal on Baldy's nose until he was satisfied it was set well enough. The hackamore arrangement would give Slocum more control, and maybe he could teach the horse how to rein.

He swung in the seat with the rope lines gathered. Baldy lifted his head and they made two passes around the corral, the horse half crow hopping and running.

"Open the gate!" Slocum shouted at her.

"Really?" she asked in disbelief, then used both hands to press the gate back for his passage.

"See you!" he shouted going by, uncertain whether Baldy would run or buck or both.

"Be careful! Come back!"

"I will!" he said over his shoulder, cut short of saying more by Baldy putting his head down again and kicking high with hind legs. The damn colt was trying new tricks on him.

Using the reins, he wrestled Baldy's head up and lashed his butt with the rope lines. The pony tore off for the south across the cleared acres, then plunged into the sagebrush sea that rolled away forever.

Slocum's eyes felt like two piss holes in the sand. Her

strong coffee had hardly cleared the cobwebs from his brain. They had spent the rest of the afternoon and night engaged in some sort of tryst. He couldn't recall ever sleeping over thirty minutes before being awakened by her mouth on his sore tool, drawing life back into it with her lips. Damn, he'd have stayed with her for certain if his conscience hadn't clawed at him over Squaw's bad situation with the baby killers.

He rode south. Kathren mentioned that the Hubbards might have a saddle horse. Their place lay fifteen miles south, and he'd hardly make it there before midday on the trotting Baldy. This game of horse and rider had begun to tire the pony, and to keep him trotting all day would probably wear out lots of rope beating his butt to make him move. Standing in the stirrups, Slocum scoped the distorted sagebrush in the heat waves. No sign of any life, or any tracks either.

Still, if they were going back to the reservation, they had to have gone south. The only ferry for miles across the Snake River was at Whistler's Post, a trading store above the fork where the Snake joined the Columbia. Whistler's was still another day's ride south of Hubbard's place by Kathren's direction. That made the two days going and two getting back that she spoke of.

Whistler's sounded like a major outpost. There might be someone there who had seen the foursome, and Slocum expected to pick up the trail there. If he managed to find a better horse at the Hubbards' place. Baldy couldn't stand another day of being pushed this hard. Already, Slocum could feel him weakening under him—a stumble over some small object and his deep breathing. He didn't want to break the colt. Lots rested on his finding another horse at the next homestead. Filled with the grimness of his task, he pushed Baldy onward.

The place's cleared land nested in a great saddle of the sage-clad sweeps. Paintless and weathered gray by the wind, dust and elements, the low-walled house, sheds and a half barn marked the welcome sight of what must be the Hubbard place. A couple of collies heralded his approach, and he felt grateful for Kathren's shave. He didn't look quite so desperate riding up toward the house. Browned stubble from the harvested wheat covered the open land; stacks of gold straw told the rest of the story.

A woman came to the door, and her dark eyes meet him with suspicion.

She was perhaps thirty, wearing a plain dress, and two small, half-dressed children clung to her legs. Her back straight, it was obvious her breasts had been suckled flat by her years of motherhood. In a knot behind her head, the silver-streaked hair was pulled tight enough to force the corners of her eyes to slant upward. An unobvious nose. Her lips were scarred white from too much sun. Defiance was written in the set of her slender jaw in the bloody light of the dying sun—Slocum held his seat on Baldy and removed his hat.

"Howdy, ma'am. Miss Kathren," he gave a head toss to the north, "said you might have a saddle horse I could buy."

Baldy put his head down and snorted wearily in the dust. The colt was through. Slocum had been forced to walk him the last half of the day, the same reason he never made this place until near dark.

"You got cash?" she asked, with a hard, inquiring look at him.

"I do." In no position to argue much with her over price, he hoped the animal she wanted to sell was sound enough to get him to Whistler's.

"He's the black in the pen. Belongs to the boy. He ain't here, but I can sell him. Go look. I've got kids to feed."

"What's he worth?"

"To you?" she asked, looking with some wariness at him. "Fifty, I reckon."

"Forty and the colt if he's sound."

"Oh, he's sound enough. Go look. You like him, we can trade."

"Yes, ma'am."

"Name's Matty."

"Slocum. Nice to meet you."

"We don't get many strangers coming out of the north. You must be pretty desperate to come from that direction."

He dismounted and undid the cinch. "Looking for three Indians, took a squaw."

She shook her head. "Never seen them. What'd she mean to you?"

"Saved my life."

"Oh. Go look at the horse. I'll rustle you some grub, if'n you ain't ate since Kathren's."

"Thanks. I'd be much obliged," he said and led Baldy toward the pen.

In the twilight, he saw the black horse eating hay at the rack. Ewe-necked and short-coupled, he'd been a stud before they gelded him. He let out a snort at the discovery of Slocum and Baldy's approach and spooked, with his eyes wide open and nostrils flared. Enough said, Slocum decided. This was one tough old codger full of surprises and spook findings.

He caught the black and felt his shins for splints. None too serious and some ringbone on his front feet—it would be years before they crippled him. The black acted and looked sound enough. Priced too high, but nonetheless, he was the best Slocum could expect. He unsaddled Baldy, turned him in the pen and left the saddle on the top bar.

He walked back to the low-walled house, accompanied by the two collies. She poured steaming water in the enamel pan set by the door and looked hard at him.

"I'll take him."

"That boy'll be proud. Get some meat and muscle on that bald-faced colt, he'd make the kinda horse that would turn some teenage girl's head."

"How old's the boy?"

"Sixteen."

"He your oldest?"

She laughed and nodded. "Oldest, yeah. Had him at thirteen under a wagon in a hailstorm. That's his name, Hale."

When he looked up, she was shaking her head in disbelief.

"He about the place?"

"Naw. He's working cattle for Erv Turrel. His pa can't stand him."

"Your husband?"

"Yeah, my husband left home at twelve and earned his keep ever since. He's hard on the boy. But you don't know Merle Hubbard and chances are you won't ever meet him."

"He's not here?"

"Naw, got the wheat up, he's off trading horses." She shook her head in disapproval and wiped her hands on her apron. "Come on in. Food getting cold."

Two small children sat on a bench in the shadows of the candlelight. Obviously, she had placed them there, for they acted frozen in place, except for their blinking eyes following his every move.

"Those your other children?" he asked, taking a seat at the table.

"Lars and Violia. Never figured I'd have another after Hale. Went ten years then Lars came and her the next."

"Nice looking."

"I wish Hale was here." She reached down and scratched her hip through the dress.

"Why's that?" he asked, cutting off a piece of browned salt pork.

"He might just ride on with you."

Slocum frowned at her, taking the meat off the fork to chew it.

"I figure Merle'll kill him before it's over."

"How's that?"

She shook her head, the white lips tight and the eyes slitted.

He chewed the green beans and waited for her to speak again. Strange how a man would even consider killing his own flesh and blood. But he'd seen father-son competition get so harsh, they ended getting into a duel or fight.

"You headed for Whistler's?" she finally asked.

"I hope to get there."

"Plenty of loose women there."

"I'm more interested in the three bucks kidnapped a squaw."

She rose and refilled the two cups with coffee. "You ain't noticed anything about them two?" She indicated the smaller children.

"No." He twisted around and looked at them. The boy was towheaded and the girl had her dark hair. They looked enough alike to be brother and sister. They spoke in low voices to each other—weren't half-wits or cross-eyed. "What's wrong?"

She shook her head to dismiss his concern. "You can't see it, then it don't matter."

"Good food." He put the two double eagle coins on the table and pushed them over to her. They gleamed in the candlelight. "Here's the money for the horse."

"It's the boy's, not mine. I'll give it to him."

"Hope him and Baldy get along fine."

"He will. He's a scrapper."

"I'm going to grab some sleep in your barn if I may and ride on. The supper was fine. If I owe you—"

She waved away his offer and walked him to the door. "There's a cot in the shed. Hale's. Sleep on it."

"Thank you again."

She clicked the two coins in his closed hand. "Yeah, thanks for dropping by."

"Yes," he said and headed for the small shed she had pointed out to him.

The door creaked when he opened it and he struck a sulfur match for light. A stub of a candle in a dish came alive with his second match. The cot had a small mattress rolled up on it and one blanket. He spread them out, set the small Colt on a chair beside the bed, then removed his shirt. Seated on the edge of the bed, he pulled off his boots and socks.

Strange woman that Matty. What was wrong with those kids? He stretched out his sour-smelling sock and wondered about her as he put it on top of his boot. No telling. The other sock off, he blew out the candle and the night closed in on the room save for the open door. He could look out at the sky full of stars—damn. He hoped he got some sleep.

"You going to wake up?" someone whispered in his ear. He realized Matty was lying on the cot with him. Half-asleep and in deep wonder, he twisted over, raised up on an elbow and blinked at her. Dressed in a billowy cotton gown, she looked very comfortable in that position.

"Why I didn't want you in the hay," she said with an edge of impatience. "Had to wait till them little ones were asleep. Sorry."

"And?"

"None of them kids are Merle's and he knows it. Why him and Hale are at war. A boy from down the road back home was Hale's pa. My pa made me marry Merle when he caught that boy and me doing it in the itchy hay. So I married him and had Hale about nine months later. But the next ten years we never had no kids. Not 'cause we didn't try. Anyway Merle was gone trading hosses. This cute cowboy about sixteen came riding by our homestead when we were in Montana.

"He hung his waist overalls on the bedpost and I had Lars. Tenth day after I had Lars, he came by to see his own flesh. Merle was gone to Billings on a trade like usual. Slocum, that tenth day works on mares. Breed them then, they'll sure stick. So did I." She chuckled and hugged his arm.

"Now you see?" she asked.

"I see. But I ain't the cute young cowboy—"

"Cute enough," she said, and rolled over toward him. She reached for his fly and undid the buttons. Her fingers closed around his limp pecker with the authority of someone in charge. "Fact, you ain't half-bad to look at."

"What if you don't—"

"Aw, don't be so particular. It don't work, think how happy you made some honyocker's dumb wife, who for a few minutes thought someone really made love to her."

He pushed the flowing gown up so his hands ran over her sharp hip bones. Then he started to slide the material higher and she caught his fingers. She pushed them to her crotch and he ran his left one through the coarse hair and into the seam.

Her mouth found his and she began to squirm, pulling harder on his stiffening poker. In seconds, he was inside her and driving his stem home in the bucking body underneath him. She drew her knees up and made a ball, rocking on her back as she cried aloud, "Go deep. Real deep."

He plunged in and out of her on top of the wads of gown. Her legs high in the air, she tried to get under him with each force to her. Then he came and she cried out.

They lay in each other's arms, the gown like a cushion between them. At last, weary of the wadded up garment, he forced her to take it off. Once it was clear of her head, he kissed the nipple on the right. She had no breasts, save the large caps, and she put her hand under it to bunch it for him.

"They never were big and breast-feeding the kids sucked them to death I guess."

"You ashamed of that?"

"A man likes titties."

"Merle say something?"

Her voice cracked. "He said doing it with me was like doing it with a boy."

With a shake of his head in disbelief, he kissed the other one. Oh, well. Who wanted to sleep anyway?

Matty fixed him a big breakfast and sent him off with some corn bread and jerky in a poke he tied on the saddle horn. He mounted the black, who flew in a whirling fit that sent Matty and the collies running for their lives. Under control, he rode over to where the two youngsters clung to her dress.

"Here," he said and tossed her a double eagle. "Buy yourself a fancy dress."

"I'll get the material next time I can get to town and I'll only wear it for you. Come back again, Slocum."

He nodded that he heard her and set the black in a trot. God bless you, Matty Hubbard, he thought.

In late afternoon, he rode off into the bottom and could see some cottonwoods along the wide river—he'd reached the Snake, and the smattering of buildings had to be Whistler's Post. He patted the short-coupled black on the neck. They were almost there. Maybe someone at the place had seen the three bucks and her.

The black stabled and grained, he headed for the store. Adjusting the small handgun in his waistband, he climbed the steps and looked over the loafer Indians seated on the porch. Then he pushed inside the store that smelled of dry goods. A pile of new brogan shoes, ready for the lacing, blocked his way to the young man wearing a white apron under the candle lamps at the counter. Slocum dodged around it and stood before him.

"Yes, sir?" the boy of perhaps eighteen said.

Slocum glanced toward the bar-restaurant to his left and the loud-voiced individual beyond the opening in the wall.

". . . the goddamn sumbitch says he can beat me at fist-fighting is lying through his teeth!"

"Who's he?" Slocum asked, looking at the revolvers under the curved glass case.

"Local farmer. Merle Hubbard and he's on a good one tonight."

"Sounds thataway. I need a good serviceable revolver. Let me see that Navy. The one with the black rubber handles."

Slocum examined it. The bore wasn't half-bad, and the distance from the cylinder to the muzzle was close. That meant the revolver wouldn't spit lots of lead sideways when he fired it.

"Some black powder, bullets and caps." Slocum motioned to the items behind the boy. "And a good used holster."

The boy took one down. Slocum examined it and nodded. "How much for all of it?"

"Ten bucks."

"Double or nothing?" Slocum asked, then frowned at the loud one next door bragging some more on his skills as a fighter.

"Afraid I can't do that, sir."

"That's fine, I'll still take it. I'll need some coffee, jerky, some sugar, and beans. A small kettle, a couple cans of tomatoes and peaches. Make it three of each and one of those canvas saddle bags. Oh, and a can of lard, too."

He loaded the .44 and capped five cylinders while the boy retrieved the goods. Then he opened the green can of lard and used a swipe to seal each loaded cylinder, so they wouldn't cross fire. Satisfied, he tried the holster, drawing and putting the gun back several times until it felt natural.

"Be thirteen dollars," the youth said, looking up after penciling down his figures on some butcher paper.

Slocum paid him with a new double eagle. "Put all that in those bags and I'll be in the bar eating. That is if that drunk will let me."

"He ain't much to picking on big guys," the clerk said softly, being certain no one else could hear his comment.

"I'll remember that," Slocum said and smiled at him as he took his change.

He paused in the doorway and saw the burly one at the bar he figured must be Matty's husband. Bent over, Hubbard appeared to be studying his glass and swearing to himself. To not evoke his anger, Slocum slipped along to the rear of the room and took a seat. The crowd at the tables was made up of mostly drummers and passersby. None looked ready or big enough to fight the big farmer at the bar who was talking tough to the bartender at the moment.

"What can I get you?" the small waiter asked, drying his hands on the cotton apron tied around his waist.

"Supper," Slocum offered. "What've you got?"

"Beef steak or lamb or salmon."

"Steak, potatoes?"

"Yeah, we got some new ones."

"There you are, darling!" Hubbard shouted and a girl about five feet tall came prancing into the room. Her beasts were barely covered by the low-cut red dress, and the slit up the side showed more leg than many husbands had ever seen. She ducked in under Hubbard's arm. Then the two turned their backs to the anxious crowd.

Obviously, Hubbard was feeling him a handful of her titties as they huddled by his drink. The edge was still on the rooms' occupants as they hurried up and ate their food while out from underneath Hubbard's scrutiny and grateful for her appearance. Several about spilled their chairs over getting up, and half ran for the door to escape anything.

Slocum tried to ignore him. The clerk brought his saddlebags, full of his purchases, and he set them in the empty chair on his right. Minutes passed and Slocum figured the novelty of the girl might keep the big bear occupied for a short while.

The waiter brought his food and hot coffee. He cut up some of the meat on his plate and was enjoying the flavorful bites.

Hubbard turned around and set his elbows on the bar, so he could eye the crowd again. A salesman obviously on a course from the back door strayed too close and Hubbard caught the man by the arm.

"Where're you going, dude?"

"Ah . . . ah . . . to my room." The man began to pale as Hubbard reached out and clasped his upper arm, holding him back.

"Hey. Me and you having a contest and she's gonna watch."

"Contest, huh?" The man shook his head to deny he wanted any part of it and looked even paler.

"Yeah, you and me."

"No—no, thanks . . ."

"Oh, yeah, we're having us a real fistfight."

Slocum rose. Without looking up and intent on laying his money down for the waiter, he spoke out loud. "Turn him loose. He don't fight bullies like you."

"And I suppose you do?"

Slocum looked up, still bent over as he turned around. Then he straightened. "Sometimes."

"Well. Ain't you the brave one there, stranger."

"Outside, both of you," the bartender said.

Hubbard waved his hand to silence the man without looking at the barman. His blue eyes tried to bore holes into Slocum. "Hold your horses, Harry. We'll go outside, 'less he's too chicken to go, but I want him to hang up that holeg first."

His arms held out, Hubbard turned around to show he had no weapons on his body.

"Fair enough," Slocum said. "The bartender can keep mine."

He walked over and handed the man the saddlebags, then the .44 wrapped in the belt. "That good enough?"

Hubbard nodded. "This is going to be your funeral, mister."

"Your opinion, Merle Hubbard."

"Hey, I never heard your name, mister."

"Didn't give it. You talking or doing something else?"

"I'm ready to tear your head off your shoulders."

Slocum held his hand out for Hubbard to go first. The big man swaggered for the door followed by the girl, who added, "You are either the dumbest fucker I ever saw or you're tougher than shit. I can't decide, mister."

"Guess we'll know that in a few minutes, won't we, darling?"

"You won't even remember this fight when you wake up," she said over her shoulder and snuggled up to the big man going out the door.

Slocum followed, and behind him came all the wide-eyed customers in the place who'd hurried to finish their food or drink so they wouldn't miss a blow. Several ordered beers to take along and came close on his heels.

He noticed all the loafer Indians were gone from the porch and Hubbard was standing in the single patch of light on the ground coming from the two open front doors. She helped him roll up his sleeves.

His eye on his opponent, Slocum handed a man at the edge of the crowd his felt hat.

"Queensbury rules?" he asked. The crowd laughed.

"Hell, we don't need no rules," Hubbard said, sparring with his fists to loosen himself up. "Man can't get up, then it's over."

Slocum nodded and completed rolling up his own sleeves. This farmer was a bear; he'd have to stay outside of his range and hammer him when he went inside. The gut might or might not be the place to attack. His head looked too thick to penetrate.

Hubbard came scuffling over, made a wild swing, and Slocum drove a barrage of fists into his gut and then was out. His adversary didn't feel that muscled in that region, Slocum thought, as he danced away from two, then three of the big man's wild punches and made two of his own to

Hubbard's face that drew a shocked expression.

"Stand still or I'll kill you!" Hubbard growled, wading in for a lucky hit.

"You said no rules." Slocum felt his breath getting quicker and his legs loosening to the toe shuffle that brought him in close and then out when Hubbard telegraphed his next try.

A haymaker missed Slocum's face by inches, but his right swing drove his knuckles into Hubbard's temple and stunned the big man. Slocum never missed a chance and drove in with a barrage of hard blows to the man's gut section, barely escaping an arm intended to pin him into a hug.

"Damn you!" Hubbard's voice was in a roar like a mad grizzly and he came, guard down, to get ahold of Slocum.

His mistake—one, two, three punches to the head drove back his attack. One solid one to the chin would have stopped an ordinary person. The big man wobbled on his feet and Slocum drove in, his hands aching with each hit until Hubbard's knees buckled. The whore screamed, "No!"

Too late, Hubbard went down. On his hands and knees, he tried to get up. He shook his head to clear it. Instead, he fell facedown in the dirt and horse manure. She rushed to save him in a wild flair of legs and skirt.

A cheer went up. "Mister, we're buying the drinks."

Slocum nodded and glanced down as he passed the fighter with his head in her lap.

"What's your goddamn name?" Hubbard asked, his right eye already swollen shut.

"Ask your wife," Slocum said. "She knows it."

He went inside, downed one free glass and excused himself. Rather than drinking the night away, he had a woman to find, and since no one at the post had seen her or her captors, he needed to move on. The black horse out of the stables, saddlebags loaded, he headed for the ferry. Maybe across the Snake they knew something.

7

"Them Injuns swim her," said the ferryboat man, who only minutes before had introduced himself in a gravelly voice as Samuel Tinsbury. With the shack's flickering candlelight dancing on his gray-streaked beard, he sat behind a table with silverware and a white china plate before him containing the remains (bread crust and bones) no doubt of his supper. His high forehead gleamed white compared to the saddle-leather tan on the rest of his face.

"Yeah, them red devils never take the ferry. Got some canoes or swim with their hosses back and forth. Course a few drown every year, but they save that ferry toll to buy whiskey and geegaws." Tinsbury chuckled and grinned foolishly back at Slocum as if he knew all the answers to all the questions.

"Your ferry got a time schedule?" Slocum asked, since the man had not offered to get up from his seat to leave.

Tinsbury shook his head. "No schedule. I was hoping someone else'd come along and I'd get two tolls. Expensive to operate a damn ferry. Takes coal, wood and repairs on the boiler. Folks don't own them don't know that."

For the sake of agreement, Slocum nodded and rubbed his sore knuckles with his left hand. Foolish to get in a fist-fight back there in the first place with someone like Hubbard—a man could break some bones in his hand. Though he doubted he'd broken any this time, still they'd be stiff and sore for several days. Maybe the big farmer had learned a lesson—he doubted it.

A nagging impatience with Tinsbury began to stir inside of him. He wanted across the Snake to see if he could pick up any tracks of the three bucks that abducted Squaw. This was day three since he'd freed himself and taken their trail. So far it had been hit-and-miss finding any trace of their movements. Standing in the small shack that reeked of tobacco, burned coal and sweaty body odors, he wondered if he should jerk the man in his rumpled clothing up by the collar and get him moving, or simply wait.

He chose the latter.

"I need me a woman." Tinsbury cupped his hands behind his head and leaned back in the straight-back chair.

Slocum acknowledged he heard the man. "Good ones are scarce."

"Yeah, had me one once. Second wife. Wasn't necessarily a good one, but she run off with a drummer that come by here. I think that sumbitch was giving her trinkets while I was across the river and he was messing with her in my absence."

"You ever catch them?"

"Naw, but she kept coming up with first, a gold locket, then a silver ring, and each time one showed up that damn drummer had been here."

"You ever ask her where they came from?"

"Said they was her mother's."

Slocum looked at the ceiling for help. He was about as interested in this conversation as he was in the price of fat hogs in Chicago.

"Yeah, she up and left me. I said, 'Louise, you can't run off with a man you don't even know.'" He paused and spat tobacco on the floor, wiped his lips on his sleeve and nodded. "But she went anyway. That's why I figure he'd been messing with her while I was across the river, huh?"

"Could have been," Slocum said and looked with relief when the man put on his floppy felt hat and rose with a loud belch.

"Cabbage done that. Every time I eat cooked cabbage, I

get the gas. Come on, just as well get up a head of steam."
Tinsbury walked bent over out the door despite the fact he
wasn't that tall.

Slocum unhitched the black from the rack and led him
down the grade to where the river slapped the sides of the
barge and tender. Tinsbury was already in the boiler room
and had the lamp lit. He soon was shoveling coal into the
boiler and grumbling as he finished with two big blocks of
wood. The metal door on the firebox shut with a clang, he
came out and stood at the rail.

"Damn stuff they call coal up here is peat. Ain't worth a
shit for heat. Got to have some wood or you'll never get up
a head of steam. Only wood's cottonwood and it don't burn
much better. Man don't own a ferry, he don't know the troubles I've got here."

Slocum paid him the four-bit toll without a comment.

"Couple bounty hunters came through here a couple days
ago." Tinsbury spat off to the side. "Better go see about the
fire."

Slocum stood by the black's head, holding the reins, in
case the start of the steam engine spooked him. A carpet of
stars overhead, he looked for the dipper and set the time as
ten o'clock. What did the old man mean "bounty hunters"?
Carter and Ward? They were the only ones he knew about
currently, but there were always some individuals prowling
around for a reward.

The steam hissed. In response, the black fell back on the
reins, his hooves pounding the hollow-sounding deck. To add
to his excitement, the paddle wheel began to spray a mist
over the two of them. Slocum patted and talked to reassure
the upset horse until at last he stood trembling in one place,
a relief to Slocum, who didn't need Black to jump overboard
into the Snake.

"What did those men want?" he shouted at the ferryman
over the noise of the steam engine and the wheel thrashing
the inky river.

"Looking for some jasper called Soo-gun. Said he was a
killer and wanted back east for murder."

"You seen this guy they wanted?"

"Lord, how would I know. There's been at least twenty men fit their description. Said he had a flashy bay horse he stole up north. Ain't seen one of them either, so I guess he swam the river, too, if'n he crossed here." Tinsbury went to chuckling to himself.

"What's so funny?"

"Was going to tell you what got me in the wife mood. A good-looking young woman last week needed across here. Had two little kids with her. Fine looker, too." In the light from the boiler room that shone on his face, he grinned like a fox and used his thumb to clean the side of his mouth. "Well, four bits is hard to come by in these hard times. Counting them little 'uns, she owed me a dollar if she came across."

"What happened?" Slocum asked to keep the conversation going in case the man said something more about the bounty hunters.

"It's why I've got to thinking about getting me a wife."

"Oh?"

"Yeah, I struck me a trade with her. Whew! I'd plumb forgot how nice it really was to rut with a female, especially a smooth-skinned one." A foolish grin parted his whiskers and the light caught the pinkish cast of his open mouth. "Wheweee! Make an old man hop around afterwards it was so durn good."

Slocum could see the dark outline of the far shore. A day or two's ride south should get him to the reservation in Oregon. Surely he could locate her there. *Squaw, I'm coming,* he thought. Another hundred yards and he wouldn't have to listen to that horny old man any more either.

8

His eyes burned to stay open. No sleep for twenty-four hours and damn little back then. He reined up Black to study the market in the too bright midday sun. The faded sign on the board nailed to the scrub pine tree said, "Cross Creek, Oregon."

He could see a church steeple, so he knew the teetotalers were already there. First thing those churchy wives wanted to do was wipe out the competition. No saloons, no gambling and no whores. Good thing they couldn't vote in most places or the West would be a vast wasteland: no place for a man to solve a thirst or a craving. Course he could drink lemonade at the church social, marry a woman of proper ways and put his small change he'd otherwise drop on a faro game or a hand of poker into the collection plate on Sunday. Good thing those old buckskinners like Jim Bridger and the rest were gone. They'd revolted over riding into some dry town with the cat houses boarded up and no gambling allowed.

He started up the street lined with stores and a two-story hotel. The saloons were still open. A few dusty hipshot saddle horses and two single-horse buggies were gathered at the hitchrail. Hoping nothing spooked Black so he broke the reins, he tied him and went inside the first one, called the Red Pony.

For a long second, he stood at the batwing doors and studied the crowd, anxious not to walk in on Carter and

Ward. He heard no familiar voices and slipped through with his eyes now accustomed to the darkness of the barroom. The bar was fancy: polished wood and mirrors beyond where the good stuff in bottles sat on the shelf.

The barkeep, a short guy in a white shirt, came over and with a rag polished the bartop, asking for his pleasure.

"Rye."

The man nodded and reached for the bottle on the shelf. He looked past Slocum once and then poured three fingers in the glass. "Better try it."

Slocum did and nodded his approval. The fiery liquor cut the trail dust going down and hit his empty stomach hard. No problem, they had the free lunch out on the side bar; he'd get him something to eat for his money.

"Be two bits."

"Leave the bottle."

"Cost five dollars for the rest of it."

"Fine." Slocum slapped the money on the bar.

What was that smell? He thought he recognized it. A strong odor in the room that had found his nose. So powerful, it penetrated his nostrils and he made a face.

"I know what you're smelling. Goddamn sheepherders," the bartender said with a sneer in the corner of his mouth. "Got to serve them, the boss says."

Slocum nodded and thanked the man. He took his glass and bottle to a place in the rear where he could have his back to the wall to survey things. Set up, he ventured to the counter and made himself two sandwiches on a wooden tray with the thin sliced roast beef, hard cheese that he cut off a large block and mustard. There were dill pickles and some other condiments. He looked in the crock and saw the pickled pigs' feet and passed on them. Overall, not a bad spread for a free one.

He ate the sandwiches slowly, catching bits and pieces of the conversations around him, his ears alert for any talk of Indians passing through. When a swarthy skinned man started past, Slocum stopped him with Spanish.

Had he seen three Indians and a squaw? One of them was riding a good dun horse.

"Ah, *sí,*" the man answered in kind. "They were camped at the edge of town this morning when I rode by them at the creek crossing to the west." He waved his hand in that direction.

"*Mucho gracias,*" Slocum said gratefully and nodded.

The sheepman returned his head bob and went back to the others at their table.

Slocum's heart quickened. If it was them, he'd gotten damn lucky. Could be any Indians. He wouldn't know until he checked them out. Finishing his sandwich became more important, and taking it in both hands, he took a man-size bite. By going over the various courses, he began to plan out a strategy on how to handle them. First, he would try taking her out of there easy-like, then when she was safe, he could settle with them. Somehow his plan didn't get past being believable with his experience. No matter, her safety came first, then the killers' apprehension—however they wanted it—dead or alive.

After finishing his lunch, he waved goodbye to the table of stinking sheepmen and the bartender before he pushed outside for a good breath of air. The whiskey bottle tucked in his saddlebag, he checked the cinch and swung into the saddle. He loosened the .44 in his holster and satisfied himself that it carried five shots. He put fresh caps on the small handgun from his boot and jammed it in his waistband. Ten shots to answer them with. Only thing better when he confronted them would be a double-barrel Greener. Somehow a twelve-gauge bore looked like a cannon on the receiving end and, in fact, opened holes in the intended target that let daylight through.

No time for another gun. He booted Black down the street, tipping his hat to some ladies on the boardwalk, and soon was by the last house and flower box. The dusty wagon tracks ran west, and he followed them toward the cotton-woods he knew lined the next water course, where they were camped last night according to the Mexican sheepherder who'd rode past them that morning. Good enough.

He could see the smoke of a cooking fire swirling low on the ground, then rising in sheets of an updraft. To move in closer on foot, he left Black tied to a box elder and made a cautious approach with the .44 rubber grips in his sweaty hand. Been better for him to try this at night when he had the cover of darkness and could give them more surprises. But his impatience to get her away from them was more powerful than his concerns about messing things up and getting her hurt.

He spotted her familiar willowy figure bent over at the fire, stirring a pot. Something caught inside his gut at the nights they'd spent together—wasted really. The youngest buck, Laughing Deer, was half-asleep, sitting with his back to a tree trunk, rifle across his lap. There was no sign of the other two, but Slocum wasn't taking any chances. He moved closer using some bushes for cover. If he could only get her attention, that was all he needed, and get her back out of the way, then he'd handle Deer. But instead of looking his way when she looked up, she looked at the horses. Bob wasn't among them that he could see. Good. Maybe Running Dog was out of camp.

Then the horses scented him and looked in his direction, and she whirled and blinked, then nodded. He started to yell for her to get out of the way.

Instead, she grabbed up her long buckskin skirt over her knees and in great strides was at Deer. Her hands reached out and jerked away his rifle, then she raised it up and slammed the butt into his skull. He fell down on his side like a poled steer.

Slocum rushed in and they began dancing in a circle holding each other, her shouting, "You came for me! You came for me!"

"Where're the others?" he asked as she pumped his hand up and down in their victory celebration.

"Gone to see Big Wolf."

"Who's he?"

"Renegade chief."

"What're their plans?"

"Burn out the settlers. Chase the white men away from here. Big Wolf says that the farmers have no guns and are cowards."

Slocum stopped dancing and nodded that he heard her. Wolf was right about the new settlers. They came to farm and claim land. Some had guns, but they were .22s and small bird shotguns, not arms for combat and protection from warring savages. This was not like the first surge of frontiersmen that came into the Northwest armed to the teeth, used to shooting Indians on sight and fighting like badgers when cornered. These were the honyockers, meek farmers—hard muscled, determined, good managers of soil and water that could wring out unbelievable crops from the volcanic ash—but still not soldiers. They'd been told the Indians in this land were drunken loafers and beggars, diggers that ran half-naked and ate grasshoppers and ants—no need to fear them unless their lice hopped on you.

"This Wolf have guns—rifles?" he asked her.

"Plenty. He been to the East and has many packhorses loaded with repeaters and bullets."

"Damn," Slocum swore and shook his head. The entire Washington-Oregon border could be on fire in no time. Someone needed to warn the military at Walla Walla and get folks that lived around there to come to town and barricade themselves in there as a fighting force, or hundreds of innocent women and children would be slaughtered. These heathens that would kill her baby would have no compassion for any other child.

"We better ride back to town and tell the local law."

She ran for a horse. He looked in disgust at the moaning Deer recovering, holding his hands to his head. Upset he must mess with Deer, Slocum took him by the arm and jerked him to his feet.

"Come on, we've got things to do."

She returned and frowned at Deer. "We take him?"

"Yes." He held his hand to stop her when she cocked the rifle and swiveled it around at him. "Can't kill him yet. He may know something more we need."

Unhappy with Slocum's idea, but obedient, she began to saddle two horses. Slocum was halfway to his black when he heard the shot and whirled in time to see Deer with a raised knife in his hand holding his gut, staggering backward. Gut-shot.

She looked at him with a sullen I-told-you-so look, put down the smoking rifle and jerked the second saddle from the horse. Slocum only shook his head and ran on for the black. Nothing he could do for Deer. They better find the town law and get folks notified.

Sheriff Tole McGrim was a squat-built man with beads of sweat popping out on his broad forehead. He used a white rag to mop it every few minutes.

"You mean to tell me that we've got renegades ready to go on the warpath?"

Slocum nodded.

"I just wrote the governor and told him there was no Indian problem in Hilton County. How long you knowed this?"

"Less than an hour. Since I found her."

McGrim gave him a look of dread. "All right, I'm sending Jerome Higgins to Walla Walla. He's part Injun, and if anyone can get through, he should, and be back in twenty-four hours." The lawman nodded for the deputy by the door to go get the man. "Then we need to scour this country and warn as many as we can. Where you figure Wolf's camp is?" the lawman asked Squaw.

"Three Forks." She used three fingers.

McGrim stood up and studied at the map on the wall until he shook his head. "There must be ten or twelve families up that drainage."

"Where are they?" Slocum asked. "She and I'll go warn them. We've got horses saddled outside. That'll save some time."

"Might get you and her killed, and this ain't even your town or county, Slocum."

"She and I'll go. Make us a rough map and show me where to look for these places. You'll run out of hands shortly sending out runners to warn folks, as many as there are."

"You're right and some won't come either," McGrim said, and looked disturbed by the knowledge.

"They get warned. We can't do much more," Slocum said.

"That's right. Here's those places." He began showing Slocum the farm and ranch locations on the wall map.

"Sheriff?" An out-of-breath man dressed in a leather shirt and canvas pants burst in the open office door.

"Get a horse saddled, Jerome. We've got renegade Injuns on the warpath. Tell that colonel at the fort we need soldiers and fast."

"How many?" Jerome asked Squaw.

"Plenty, maybe three moons."

"That's a hundred. Wow, that many?" Jerome asked her again, shaking his head in disbelief.

"Got plenty."

"Whew, I'll ride over there and tell him, but I sure hope she's right." Jerome looked at McGrim and Slocum for his answer.

"She's right," Slocum added, "and she knows they've got new rifles for all of them and ammo."

Jerome scratched his beard. "Them Cayuse never liked being put down there with the Nez Percé. I ain't surprised."

"Get tracking. Sooner you get that ole colonel going, the less lives we stand to lose," McGrim said.

"I'm going. Got my fast horse. Be back here with the Army's word in twenty-four hours."

McGrim followed the man to the door, giving him more instructions. Slocum studied the map of the basin.

McGrim returned to his desk, where he scribbled on a list with a lead pencil. "Them folks won't want to leave their places, but they better. Hardest one for you to get out will be Milo Stone. He's a tough old cuss, got a young woman with four little kids, too. Cowski won't come either. Hell, he's knuckleheaded as a billy goat, but he's also an old Indian fighter. They might've bit off more than they can chew. Good luck, Slocum. I listed them like you'll find them. The first names are on the right side of the basin. Cowski is last—he's far down on the south end, farthest one."

The lawman showed Slocum the list and he stuck it in his vest pocket. "We'll do what we can. I know about stubborn folks."

"I appreciate this. You need a rifle?"

"How about a shotgun?" Slocum asked.

"Help yourself. Jarvis, get him some of them brass shells, too." McGrim handed the shells to her and made a wary face at Slocum before he spoke. "You two be careful. Way I figure it, you're running right into their jaws."

Slocum nodded and gave her a head toss that he was ready to leave.

"Here," McGrim said and tossed him a badge from the drawer. "You may need this to prove you're for real."

Slocum nodded, then slipped it in his upper vest pocket. "I may."

They two left town in a short lope. He looked off toward the blue-tinted hills and the direction they must ride. *Into the jaws of the enemy.* That's where they were headed.

9

A woman in a sun-bleached dress that buttoned down the front suspiciously eyed them from the porch. She used the side of her hand to shade her eyes and try to make them out better in the mid-morning glare.

"Mrs. Cannon?" Slocum asked.

"Yes, who are you?" Still wary acting, she folded her arms and shot arrows at Squaw.

He flashed the badge and put it back in his vest pocket. "I'm a deputy sent out here to warn you that several Cayuse renegades are on the warpath. Sheriff McGrim would like for you and the children to move into town until the Army can round them up."

"Hmm," she snorted out her long slender nose as she stood contemplating his words. Her face was red; she was someone who obviously never tanned. Her brown hair hung limp and the ends were uneven from the last scissor cutting. She looked more perplexed by the minute over the information.

"Mister, we ain't had no Injun trouble since we come here. Why now?"

"Ma'am, we need to ride on, but I can guarantee you there will be Injun trouble in the next few days, maybe within twenty-four hours. Only place that you and these children will be safe is in town."

"I'll tell my man when he comes in. What she's got to do with it?" She motioned to Squaw.

"She's the one that warned us." He started to turn Black to leave. There were eight others up this basin who still needed to be warned.

"You better go to town," Squaw said as she rode up toward her. "They murdered my baby."

The woman's hands flew to her face in shock and her brown eyes widened. "Oh, dear God, I'm sorry."

Squaw accepted her words with a nod and they rode on.

McCarty was the next name on the list, and in an hour they short loped their sweaty horses up a long lane with a post-and-rail fence on both sides. The peeled log house was a two-story, and a passel of dogs came out to meet them with throaty barks.

A man stepped out of a shop; obviously, from the smell of burning coal, he was working at blacksmithing and the fire was in his forge.

"Morning," he said when Slocum showed him the badge.

"The sheriff wants you to get your women and children to town. There are armed Cayuse renegades expected to raid this basin. Until the Army can get them rounded up . . ." Slocum continued his plea, and the man was joined by a concerned-faced woman and several small children at her skirt tail.

"What'll we do, Mac?" she asked her man.

"Get some things. I'll hitch a team and we'll go to Cross Creek. Get what we need ready."

"But—our house? Our things?"

"Our lives first," he said.

Slocum nodded in approval. "Best get going, too. They're well armed and angry, according to the reports."

"Thanks, mister. I never caught your name."

"Slocum."

"Nice to meet you." He waved as the two of them rode on.

The next name marked was Terry. That would make three of nine so far. They rode up a canyon fed by a small stream, and the smell of smoke told him the cabin was close.

They discovered a raw, low-walled cabin set back in the hillside.

A man came out the front door with a Hawkins rifle in his arms. His face was a mask of gray-black whiskers with a corncob pipe in the left-hand corner of the concealed mouth. His filthy overalls had one knee torn out, and the collar of his shirt was unraveled. His raven black eyes didn't miss a thing, including Squaw.

"What's your business?" the man asked sharply.

"The Cayuse renegades are freshly armed and on the war-path, Mr. Terry. Sheriff McGrim wants all the women and children taken into Cross Creek until the Army can round them up."

"Get out here, bitch!" he shouted over his shoulder.

A short Indian girl, very much pregnant judging from her swollen belly, soon came to the door, with her head bowed submissively.

"They won't bother me. I've got me one of them. What ya take for yours? I could kinda take a shine to her ass." He used his rifle barrel to indicate Squaw.

"Not for sale. Stay here at your own risk, Terry."

"That fucking McGrim never done me no favors in his life. Surprised he even sent you all that way out here."

Slocum nodded. "So am I." With a head toss, they turned their horses and left. That turkey could rot in hell for his money.

"Whiskey man," she said from behind him when they were a quarter mile from the place.

"I smelled the sour mash. He's got a batch coming off. That may be the thing fires those renegades off, too."

"What we do about it?" she asked, catching up on her horse.

"When we get everyone warned, if there's time we can come back and see about blowing it up."

"Good." She smiled, pleased, and they trotted their horses south for the Summersets, next on his list.

The whitewashed frame house sat in a yard of rambling roses and climbing sweet pea vines that covered the picket fence. Slocum dismounted, scratched the wooly, reddish brown stock dog behind the ear and opened the gate. She held the horses and looked over the neat pens and corrals.

"Good day, sir," a straight-backed woman in her thirties with pinned-up graying hair said, stepping out on the small porch. Her red checkered dress looked freshly ironed and was tailored to her willowy form, with lace at the cuffs.

"Mrs. Summerset?"

"No, I'm Lenore. What may I do for you?"

He showed her his badge and went to explaining the situation.

She nodded that she understood but showed no alarm or concern. "May I make the two of you some tea?"

"No, thanks. Who else lives here?"

"Dewayne, my brother, and his son, Alex. Sorry, but they are logging in the hills. I don't expect them back till late in the day."

"Do you have a buggy horse?"

She nodded.

"Then drive it to Cross Creek. This is a serious matter."

"But what about—"

"Leave them a note. These renegades are armed and will be on the warpath. Now, will you please drive to town this afternoon?"

"Yes, sir," she said submissively. "I'll consider it."

"Then we must ride on and warn the others."

"Thank you, sir."

"Slocum," he said and touched his hat.

"Where's her man?" Squaw asked quietly.

"Up in the hills cutting wood."

Squaw shook her head in disapproval and they headed out for the next place.

Slocum hoped the woman did as he told her. This job of being a messenger wasn't much fun when folks balked at doing what they needed to do. No telling who would and wouldn't get out. But he'd have less on his conscience after he told them about the menace.

The Marleys were in the hay field eating lunch on a blanket. A burly man in his forties brushed off the seat of his britches and strode over to meet them. He nodded underneath his straw hat when Slocum showed him the badge and began to explain the situation.

"They really that tough?" he asked. "All I ever seen was some laying around in town and stumbling around drunk."

"No, Marley, these have repeating rifles and they'll be vicious with anything in their path. McGrim sent for the Army, but they won't be here for few days anyway."

"What is it?" a mature-bodied woman asked, tossing a errant wave of her reddish-brown hair aside from her face as she joined them.

In the saddle and looking down at her as she came in a swinging walk to join her husband, Slocum could visualize her well-developed body without the dress. Globe-size breasts, smooth ample hips—a womanly enough form to take a man's breath. Marley better take his advice and move her and the young children with pitchforks to Cross Creek if he treasured them.

"I'll take them there," he said and turned to his wife. "Dallia, we need to load the wagon and all of us go into town. The deputy here says the Cayuse are on the warpath."

"Warpath?" Her tanned face blanched, then with her full lower lip underneath her even underteeth, she began to round up her brood.

"Never caught the name," Marley said.

"Slocum."

"We'll be on our way in the hour if you're sure?"

"McGrim has everyone he could find out warning folks to come in. He figures we can hold them off there in town against anything they can throw at us. The Army will be here in a few days. That will change things."

"I understand."

Slocum nodded to both of them and they rode on.

They found Dawson with his sheep. He stood on a high knoll and waved his hat to them with a sharp whistle to get their attention. Sheep lifted up their heads at their passing, and bleating lambs ran about looking for a chance to get some teat. Their dam's front legs straddled apart to get them under her belly, and the lambs pulled and butted the source until she became tired of the abuse and drove them off the handle with a kick or butt.

A pair of black-and-white collies came to greet them as they reined up.

Dawson took off his weathered hat and nodded for the two of them. He leaned on his wooden staff and smiled.

"And what brings the likes of you up here?"

Slocum showed him the badge and began, "Serious business."

"Aye and what would that be, laddie?"

"Bad troubles with the Cayuse renegades," he started, going on to explain the problem.

"Land's sake, I can't leave me sheep." The man's blue eyes bore a hole in Slocum as he reined up the black to make him be still.

"My job isn't to make your decisions. I'm here to tell you the forces of hell could come down this basin any moment. You might not need any sheep when they get through with you."

"And I'm beholden to ya, laddie. But no thanks, I'll stay here." Hearing the resolution in his words, Slocum nodded and turned the black to leave. "Keep an eye pealed. They won't be coming up to beg tobacco this time."

"I understand," Dawson said and nodded solemnly. "And a good day to you, too, there pretty one." Then he smiled for her.

Quickly, she nodded at him, looking embarrassed at the man's words. With her reins, she turned her bay to leave with Slocum.

When they had ridden a ways from the sheepman, Slocum laughed. "You look into his eyes?"

She glanced back and then smiled at him. "No mustang man, but him good one."

"You ain't a half-bad judge of folks, I'd say. Only thing, he may not survive this deal, if he stays up here."

She nodded and slapped her horse with the reins to make him trot faster.

They were three miles from the sheep herd and headed

up the main floor of the basin when he spotted dust from riders coming in their direction. He tossed his head to the cover of some box elders, and they rode aside to hide, wait and see who passed.

Standing beside their horses to control them whining to the passersby, they watched the four riders in war paint gallop north. Slocum pulled out his brass telescope. In the lens he saw the bright, new repeaters they carried in their hands. After he saw them, he passed the telescope to her.

"Tall Horse," she said, peering through the eyepiece. "One they call Bear Gone, and two boys."

"I didn't see Running Dog with them."

She shook her head and collapsed the column before handing it back. "Him must be with Wolf."

"Wonder what those four were after." He wished for the rifle McGrim had offered. The Greener in his scabbard would never have dropped them at the distance when they passed. But a good .44–40 and he would have taken at least two of them down—hindsight always won out over common sense. No need to cry over spilled milk; he couldn't even sponge it up. Besides they were gone to join the others.

She shrugged.

"Will they need more horses?"

"I don't know . . ."

Damn, they still had folks to warn and they already had Injuns swarming like angry hornets in the basin. He nodded to her. "They're gone. Let's ride."

10

Their hard-breathing, sweaty horses needed to be walked when they closed the distance between them and the cabin on the rise. Bacon was the name scribbled on the list, beside an x on the west side of the basin. Looking around, Slocum felt they were there. Something white that looked like one-piece underwear on the clothesline snapped and whipped in the fresh wind. Halted before the place, Slocum handed her the reins and they shared a frown when he stepped down. The front door stood open, and he expected any moment someone to step into the frame. He reached the steps and his hand went for the butt of the .44. Something tightened his feelings and he wondered what was wrong.

Then he stood in the doorway and the bloody sight on the floor told him—*too late*. On the floor lay a woman—he recognized a blue dress still twisted around her scarlet body. It took a deep breath to steady him. Her attackers had raped her and then no doubt cut her to ribbons. He rushed to the bed and found a feed-sack sheet the raiders had dropped, and grateful for it, he hurried back with the bed linen to cover the hideous sight of their immense cruelty from his vision. On his knees, he rolled what was left of the woman in the cloth and then forced himself up on his feet.

She stood guard in the doorway holding the greener ready, looking over the country they came from. He brushed past her and outside in the too bright sunshine; he threw up. The sour, rotten smell flooded his nostrils and made his eyes run.

"Jesus, girl, I'm not up to this." He gritted his molars to gain some control, still expecting more to upchuck; then when none came, he wiped his mouth on his kerchief, straightened and shook his head.

"Dog did this," she said. Her eyes were hard slits and her ripe breasts rose and fell under the buckskin shirt with each breath.

"See any tracks?" he asked.

"Four horses." She pointed to the ground in the yard cut up by horses being charged around.

"Any sign of children or a man? This damn paper just gives a last name. No information." He drew in a deep breath for strength. "You keep an eye out. I'll go look around."

The stalls doors in the log barn were thrown open and he walked the shadowy alleyway to the back door, to see a jersey cow lying dead, her body a pincushion full of arrows, beside her a milk-fat calf gutted. No doubt they'd eaten his heart and liver raw. No sign of any horses. He went back inside the barn's interior, headed for the house, and noticed a pitchfork standing up in the center of a stall. Filled with dread, he stepped through the stall gate, his eyes adjusted to the dim light. On the floor, he saw the ivory naked body of the man, the pitchfork stabbed into his back to the hilt. The sight jolted his own heart—how long ago? They must have been only a few hours too late. His eyelids forced shut to get the sight from his vision, he tried to spit away the foulness in his mouth. A shudder racked his frame and he began coughing.

Forced to go out of the stall, he jammed his shoulder to the rough board wall. Damn senseless killings, anyway.

When he'd recovered some of his composure, he looked up and saw Squaw in the backyard. Something else was wrong.

"They threw the children bodies in the well," she said, indicating the rock wall and bridging to pull up the bucket.

He closed his eyes and nodded he had heard her words. How much more would they do? That was only four killers.

"How many will ride for this Wolf?"

"Maybe two, three moons."

She knew how to count by the days in a lunar month. He wouldn't doubt her numbers. They needed to go find this man McGrim said wouldn't heed his warnings. He dug out the list. Stone, then Cowski.

"Get the horse. We'll have to come back and bury them later."

"I tell you to kill them?" she asked quietly.

"Yes, you said I might have to."

"Big shame, you no kill 'em." She hurried off in a flurry of leather fringe.

"I thought that when they killed little Wayne." The words tumbled from his numb lips, but she was gone too far to even hear him. He looked across the basin to the far, blue-cast mountains. "Been reminded a hundred times, too, since then, I guess."

Stone's place was watered by a small creek. The small patch of alfalfa looked verdant green and ready to cut. They rode up the lane and dogs barked, a sign that stirred Slocum. Perhaps they were there in time. Wide-eyed children ran to report the strangers to the woman who soon appeared drying her hands as she came to study the intruders.

"Hello, Mrs. Stone?" He spoke to the pregnant woman. The big bulge in her belly strained the wash-worn material of her faded dress.

"Aye—oh, I see you're a lawman. Good day to you, too," she said to Squaw.

"Is your husband here?"

"Course I'm here." The voice soon proved to be from an untrimmed, gray-shot beard and a burly man of five-six as he rounded the corner of the house. He looked more like a great ball, and when he swept off his hat, his bald head shone with beads of sweat.

"Sheriff McGrim sent me to warn you . . ." Slocum began, telling the man his business.

"Well, we ain't leaving."

"Mr. Stone, could you and I talk a moment in private?"

Slocum waited for the man's reply. At the nod, he dismounted and handed Squaw the reins to the black.

As the two started around the house, one of the children asked, "What's he talking to Pa about?"

"Never mind, Herschel. You kids stay here and be quiet."

"I know you have lots of hard work here and don't want to leave it—"

"I ain't leaving it for no goddamn blanket-ass Injun scare."

"This ain't a scare. They murdered Bacon not two hours ago. Raped and cut up his wife so bad I tossed up my guts. Then they brutally killed his children and threw them in a well. Do I make myself clear?"

"Did all that at Bacon's?" he asked in a small voice.

Slocum nodded.

"I'll take them to Cross Creek."

"Now?"

His eyes full of dread, the man nodded. "Right now."

"You can replace things. Not lives." Slocum clapped the man on the shoulder of his threadbare suit coat. "You won't regret it."

"Oh, I will, but a man my age won't get a third chance. Lost my first family to cholera. I was forty-seven when I found Mary and we've got four fine ones, looking for five." Stone looked off at the faraway range. "I won't get another chance—I'll be there."

"We're going to Cowski's. Should meet you on the road in two hours. Be careful. We almost rode into one band. There should be others. Get in a train. Have your guns ready."

"I'll leave a rag on a bush when we come out, so you don't have to ride up here."

"Thanks," Slocum said and shook the man's hand. He hurried around in front and took the reins from Squaw. He saluted the missus and started to leave.

"Hey, mister," a young boy called out, holding a hand up to shade the high sun. "What did you tell my pa?"

"He'll tell you, son. He's coming now."

"He told me we were all going to town for a few days," Stone said, coming around the building.

"But—"

"No. Mary, get your things in the wagon. We're going."

Slocum turned the black and they rode for the last name, Cowski.

An hour later, their horses churned up dust approaching some corrals and pens. Slocum stood in the stirrups and looked for signs of anyone. The headquarters looked like a typical cow outfit, and somehow for him that didn't match the Polish-sounding name on his list. Still, he hadn't seen a sign of a human yet.

Then he spotted three paint horses and shouted for her to get down. On the ground, he ripped the shotgun out of the scabbard and tossed it to her. She caught it and broke it open, took two brass shells from her dress pocket, loaded the gun and snapped the breech shut.

Waving the Colt in his hands to indicate the paints, Slocum ran low along the pens. She came on his heels. When they reached the end, he waved her back and peered toward the low-walled shack with the rusty stovepipe sticking out of the shingle roof. On the ground between him and the structure were three bodies—no doubt from their black hair and the blankets around their waists, they were dead Indians.

"Cowski, you there?"

No answer.

"Cowski?" he called louder.

"Yeah, whose out there?"

"A deputy sheriff and an Injun woman."

A crackly laugh came from the shack. "That's different. Come on over. I think all them red-balled niggers is dead. They ain't twitched in the last hour."

Slocum straightened and drew a deep breath. She hurried to join him, both of them searching around for any survivors.

"You know them?" Slocum asked under his breath as they hurried by the sprawled corpses.

"One is Wolf's son—Silver Wolf."

"Oh, that's nice."

"What's nice?"

"One of them is the big chief's son," Slocum said as the

short man came outside the half-underground house.

A bandy-legged man hardly five-six, his face wrinkled like old leather from ten thousand days in the broiling sun—a graying mustache under a big nose that looked like a long-horn steer rack and the clearest blue eyes—stood with an oily looking repeater in his hands.

"Sonsabitches, they came to die today, boy."

"Cowski?"

"That's me."

"Sheriff McGrim sent me to ask you to come to Cross Creek."

"What in God's name fur?"

"Wolf's got a large band of renegades and they all have new repeaters."

"Yeah, these pups had them rifles. They couldn't hit a bull in the ass with one."

"Still, sixty rifles might."

"About even the odds—hell, I'm sorry, never noticed her." He removed his wide-brimmed hat that dipped from the elements all the way around his small head. Swiftly, he made a bow at the waist toward her, and his great Mexican rowels jingled.

"You're prettier than the bluebells down in Texas in the spring, little lady. I once lived with an Injun woman in a dugout in the Indian Nation. Guess I'd still be down there with her, but some whiskey trader rode by the dugout one day I was gone and he murdered her."

Slocum nodded that he heard the man.

Cowski's clear eyes narrowed and his mouth opened; his teeth fit together and he trembled. Then his hat was back on, covering his thin thatch, and he spoke low and soft. "The things I did to that worthless piece of shit never paid her back for his mercilessly killing some of the finest she stock to ever dance across the prairie grass. Dammit, you rode a long ways for nothing, Slocum, is it?"

"Yes. What can one man do here?"

"I killed three so far. The next ones come, I've got those three's rifles and mine, two Colts full of lead, and a ten-gauge shotgun. And a box of dynamite for anyone dumb enough to come in that cave and see if this old sumbitch is dead yet."

"They've already got the Bacon family."

"Good folks, but they never knew Comanches. Good thing these Cayuse never took no lesson from them Comanches I fit back in Texas. Hell, you ain't seen Injuns till you match up with a Comanche. They're more like smoke than humans."

Cowski wiped his mouth with his hand. "They got my second woman."

Slocum nodded. Squaw had gathered all their rifles and had them leaned against the horse rack. In minutes, she returned with their horses and undid the cinches.

"Good woman," Cowski said in approval, watching her work. "Come on, I've got some fresh coffee. 'Fore you ride off and tell McGrim that damned fool Cowski up there is staying put, have a cup and we can palaver."

Slocum nodded.

"You, too, little lady. Come have some coffee." He headed for the cabin in his rolling bowlegged gait, with his spur rowels clinking like little silver bells.

Privately, she grinned at Slocum and nodded after the little man that she approved of him. Then with her chin held high, in a whirl of fringe and leather, she came beside Slocum and joined in his steps. He reached over and squeezed her shoulder.

Slocum wanted to laugh aloud—she'd already looked into that old rancher's eyes.

After his coffee, Cowski loaned Slocum four sticks of dynamite, caps and fuses. Those secure in his saddlebags, Slocum thought about her money in there that he intended on returning to her. They mounted up. Slocum planned to ride into town and fill the sheriff in on the Bacons' deaths and his progress with the others. Also to check on things as they went back and see if any of the folks on the road needed any help. Perhaps if they made a train, those people could defend themselves better.

"You don't let no damn drunk bucks bother her none," Cowski said and waved after them.

"I won't. You keep your scalp, too," Slocum added and booted his black northward.

"Don't worry about me none. They won't get a hair of it without a fight."

They rode out.

"The money," Slocum said when they were out of hearing. "I have it. It's yours. I used some to get here."

She nodded, riding stirrup to stirrup with him. "You keep."

"Ain't mine. You'll need it." He looked at her for a reply.

She nodded but made a sign with her hand that the money was fine with him. He found no reason to argue at that point. His gaze searched the pine-clad hills, looking for any smoke that might signal another raid.

"You reckon that Horse was going after whiskey when he rode by us?" he asked.

"Maybe."

"Only person that would have whiskey going in that direction would be Terry, right?"

"He have it."

"He's sold it to Indians before, hasn't he?"

"Yes. How he got that Cayuse girl."

"Traded whiskey for her?"

Her eyes set in slits, she nodded. "Goddamn whiskey, bad stuff."

Slocum agreed and booted Black into a lope. "We better hurry."

They crossed lots of ground. They found Stone's white flag that said they were on their way. Slocum could see the marks of several wagon tracks on the main road. Good—folks were headed for Cross Creek, so they hadn't run into those four bucks. He believed they were responsible for the Bacon family's demise, though he could prove little and had less time for an investigation. He knew from the brutal way Tall Horse killed Little Wayne that he had no compassion for life. Savages of some kind did it, anyway.

In a short while, they caught the Marleys' wagon. He was driving, and a teenage boy of perhaps sixteen rode one and led one saddle horse. On a bed piled with food and bedding, the three younger ones waved at them

Marley drew up. "How's you's effort going?"

Slocum shook his head. "Not the best. They've already struck at the Bacons'."

"Oh, not Jane—" the missus said and bit her lower lip.

"Sorry, but the news isn't good. Four bucks rode down this valley a few hours ago. Ma'am, you need to hold that rifle ready for 'em. Don't ask any questions. Shoot them."

"What if—"

"Sorry. As inhumane as it sounds—go to shooting."

Marley nodded, but acted unconvinced.

Slocum reined the anxious, hard-breathing black closer and looked squarely at the man. "I didn't kill them once. They returned and murdered this woman's baby."

"I'll take you at your word," he said and drew the rifle up to hand to his wife.

"Don't take a chance. Come on," he said to Squaw and they hurried northward.

"That man did not want to kill them?" Squaw asked, over the drum of their horses' hooves.

"Killing a man ain't easy when you've spent your whole life trying not to kill anyone."

"I see. I could kill them. If I had a gun when they held me prisoner, I would have killed them. But they never left me alone. They knew I would, too."

Slocum looked off to the blue-cast hills and nodded. The fact he hadn't done it back then niggled his conscience again. They reached Terry's cutoff in late afternoon. Riding up, she pointed to the unshod pony tracks and he nodded.

Only one thing wrong. The tracks went in and they didn't come out. Tall Horse had had plenty of time already to barter for the whiskey and be back out if that was the plan. The notion that Slocum had was that once those four had the liquor, they'd gone back up the basin to where Wolf and the main party of renegades were situated. There mighty be something else going on—damn.

11

"Have'um big party down there," Squaw said, looking away from the eyepiece of the brass telescope.

"There's more than four renegades, too," he said, bellied down beside her as they overlooked the Terry place. Timber obscured seeing everything going on, but he could count lots of war-painted bodies.

"Must be thirty or more."

No way that Squaw and he could handle that many drunk Indians. Plus Terry. He had yet to catch sight of the whiskey trader, but he was somewhere down there where the hooting and dancing was going on. Scratch his plan to capture Tall Horse and those other three killers. He plucked a stem of grass to chew on. Next effort—probably go to Cross Creek and talk to the sheriff.

How far away was the Army? Days? No way to know. The military could be swift or hidebound to regulations that required a presidential order to come down even to save civilian lives. Sometimes the Army's animals were ill supplied by profiteers and a snail could outdistance them, even to the point where they turned cavalry units into infantry outfits because of the remount problems. He could hope those in service at Walla Walla were better equipped.

He began to slip back down the slope a ways from the rise. She did the same. In the draw, they ran bent over, going for their horses concealed in the timber. It would be dark in an hour, maybe less—the flaming sun was ready to drop under the horizon.

"Where we go now?" she asked as he tightened his latigos.

"Find us someplace to den up for the night. Come first light, we'll ride for town."

"Good," she said and slipped aboard her pony. Slocum was about ready to mount his when the hair on his neck bristled. His hand shot to the gun butt; his fist grasped the grips.

"Get down," he hissed at her. From the corner of his eye, he caught sight of her obeying him. In one fluid motion, he spun on his heels and cocked the Colt at the same time, shoving it forward ready to shoot at the first thing that moved.

"Wait!" Squaw said and ran to the Indian girl coming through the timber. All she wore was a leather blouse that barely covered the round ball of her extended belly. Her bare legs were scratched and bleeding. Her face looked battered, too.

Squaw caught her in her arms and looked up at Slocum. "They hurt her."

"This the girl at Terry's?" He took the limp form in his arms, looking into her face with the purple bruise under her right eye.

"Yes, her name is Yellow Bird."

"She's coming around. Ask her who did this." Her eyes were half-open, but she looked exhausted.

Squaw spoke in tongue to her. The girl answered in broken sentences until at last she closed her eyes again.

"She says Tall Horse and all his bucks raped her 'cause Terry not there to sell the whiskey when they came."

"Is Terry there now?" He shifted her weight in his arms.

"Yes, he come home and she get chance to run away."

"They may come look for her. Lead that black over by the rock and I'll get in the saddle with her. Damn bastards. What next?"

"She said they bragged about raping a white woman, too."

He closed his eyes. "Must mean Mrs. Bacon. Bird's

lucky—they didn't cut her all up. They're might handy with a knife."

In the saddle again, Squaw led the way in the growing twilight. The girl he held mumbled something, but he figured it could hold. There were smells of her that filled his nostrils, of sweaty men, fishy tainted seminal fluids, campfire smoke, earthy dirt aromas and her own sour perspiration that no doubt once had been tinged with fear. Hardly bigger than a child, he guessed her age as mid-teens. Most Indian girls by fourteen were married and pregnant; at thirty-five, they were wrinkle-faced, stooped over from all the work, and expecting the younger wives to do their work for them.

They rode until the Big Dipper filled the sky and he told her to stop. She dismounted and ran over in the starlight to take his burden. In the process, Bird awoke and with Squaw's help stood on sea legs. The warmth on the spot where she had lay across his legs and belly quickly evaporated. He stretched his stiff arms over his head and yawned. A few hours' sleep and they could ride on again.

Not much chance the drunken Cayuse would track them. Squaw delivered a blanket to him.

"I better stay with her," she said, sounding disappointed.

Slocum agreed. "She need anything to eat?"

"No, she is too upset about what those men did to her."

"Got a good reason to be upset. Let's only sleep a few hours here." His finger undid the latigos and he soon stripped off the saddle.

"Squaw's work," she said, shaking her head in disapproval at him, and went back to be with the girl.

When Black was hobbled, he flung open the blanket and settled down on a mattress of pine needles. Somewhere to the north a wolf howled, another answered.

His arm for a pillow, he soon went off into dreamland. He rode a long-headed bay horse. In the distance he could see lots of smoke. Cooking fires—couldn't be that many individual ones on the Little Bighorn River. Perhaps the hostiles had set the prairie on fire. No telling—hotter than the seven shades of hell. Captain McEvoy said his mercury thermometer had registered a hundred-six the day before.

No sign of Terry or Crook. Best he had overheard was the three columns were to meet here by driving all the wild Indians into the basin. Crook to come from the south and Terry from the north, with Custer's command in the center. This would trap all the renegades in the rich buffalo country between the Powder and the Big Horns. And if nothing else, simply keep the hostiles on the move and not letting them hunt for food supplies would keep them from ever coming onto the reservations and surrendering.

Cheyennes were out there somewhere—Crazy Horse's band. The fierce one, and the great Sioux medicine man Sitting Bull, were in this vicinity, plus a dozen Sioux war chiefs. Throw in a handful of Arapahos to make things more spine tingling. But the worst part was the loose ground—a thousand travois poles must have been dragged over this land and mulched it, for one could sow wheat and then use a light harrow and disk it in for a crop. Except in this broiling heat and drought, nothing would ever come up.

"Slocum, Major Benteen wants to see you, at once."

"I'm on my way," he said to the sergeant.

"No hurry, they're fixing to take on a big camp of them red niggers ahead."

"Serious? Without Terry and Crook?"

"You know the man by now. Custer ain't leaving no glory to them bastard boys."

Slocum nodded and booted his horse to the head of the company. Then they were in the river bottom—up sprang ten thousand Indians to greet them, armed with bows and arrows, six-guns, old rifles, repeaters and tomahawks. The bugle sound soon came to retreat as men fell like stems of wheat in a sickle bar binder.

On the ridge, at last, with the wounded men moaning in the night, he lay on his belly hoping to see any attacker coming from the camp below. Reno's supply train along with them was cut off from joining Custer or knowing his fate. Belly down atop a waterless ridge, on a hellish day in late June 1876—Slocum thought he would die in that place, but he didn't.

He sat up in his blanket, bathed in his own sweat. A night

wind drew goose bumps on the backs of his arms. It wasn't wounded men moaning he heard; it was Bird crying aloud and Squaw trying to comfort her in the starlight.

Bird rode double behind Squaw, and they set out for town in the predawn. When they found the road, they discovered two wagons in a caravan—Lenore and the two Summerset men as well as the Marleys.

"No sign of them Injuns," Marley said, cradling the rifle in his arm. "Took turns guarding camp all night."

"Good," Slocum said and dismounted. "There's a couple dozen or so last night getting liquored up at Terry's."

"That sumb— Selling them whiskey?" the older Summerset asked. He shook hands with Slocum. "Dewayne's mine and my boy, Alex."

Slocum nodded to the slender, dark-haired boy of eighteen. He noticed that Squaw had talked Mrs. Marley out of some clothes for Bird. She and Lenore fussed over the young woman.

"Marley said you told him to live with his guns?" Summerset asked.

"Need to. That bunch at Terry's could get fortified with that hooch and come screaming down on you all in no time." He turned and looked to the southwest. No telling, but they were probably still several hours from Cross Creek.

"You really think that Terry sold them firewater?" Summerset made a frown.

"Sold it or what I'm not sure. That dozen bucks raped that Indian girl there that was living with Terry 'cause he wasn't there when they got there. She got away from them. But them renegades were having a war dance down at Terry's when Squaw and I left that country."

"She say anything about them?"

"When twelve bloodthirsty bucks raped you, there isn't much to say. We found Bacon and his wife and family murdered."

"Her, too?"

Slocum nodded. "It was such a bad scene when I wrapped her in a sheet, I puked."

"Who else?"

"Stone should be in town already. The sheep man refused to leave his flock. Cowski is denned up at his ranch. Only ones I can't account for."

"But they got the Bacons?" the man asked, as if that wasn't even true.

"Yes, we need to get these women and children on into town."

"Slo-cum!" Squaw shouted and pointed to some dust.

It was riders and they were coming from the northeast, not from Cross Creek.

"Everyone get their arms. We better turn over the wagons for cover—there's no time for a run for it."

"Squaw, take my black and ride for the hills. Then you circle back and tell the sheriff we're under attack. Ride, girl. Bird will be fine here. You ride."

She ran to the horse, took the four sticks of dynamite out and whirled to hand them to him as he caught up. "These may make a difference. Be careful."

His hands full, he leaned over and kissed her. His effort brought a warm smile to her face.

In an instant she was on the black and racing for the timber. Good enough head start—she should be back with help in a few hours if they could hold out.

"Everyone help turn over these wagons," Summerset shouted, and they rushed to the Marley rig. In seconds, it was on its side. Slocum set down the dynamite, jerked the shotgun out of Squaw's scabbard and handed it to Mrs. Marley. Then he cut the leather strings and freed her saddlebags with the shotgun shells in them. He waved at their fleeing loose horses to hurry them away. One check of the approaching war party and he handed Mrs. Marley the bags. "Shells are inside. It's not a long gun, but close it is a good one."

She looked hard at him, holding the scattergun as if it were some strange object.

He paused. "This you have to do."

She gave him a weak nod. "This I must do?"

"Must do."

"I will."

"Thanks." He wanted to say a thousand things more. Like

how he admired her ripe form, how beautiful he thought she was. How war was hell and killing people the worst part. But there was no time. Summerset was calling for help—his wagon was too heavy to turn over.

"Unlock the bolsters and slide the box off the side," Slocum directed. "Get the food and water in the center. And go to digging pits in there, too."

Both wagon boxes were on their sides ten feet apart. Marley, the Marley boy Able, Alex, Dewayne and himself made five men.

"Can either of you shoot?" Slocum asked the two women.

"I'm a fair shot," Lenore said.

"Mrs. Marley—"

"Dallia."

"Dallia, you reload rifles. Bird!"

The Indian girl turned to listen. "You watch those two little children. Make them stay down." He pointed to the Marley kids and used his hand to show her how to shove their heads down.

She nodded and the dirt was flying. Slocum climbed up on the wagon box to look things over. Squaw was already out of sight in the timber. Good. He had one Winchester. He reached down and drew it up by the barrel, levered a cartridge in the chamber and sighted down the barrel. Through the billowing dust, he saw the war paint and feathers.

"How deep?" Marley asked, making a groundhog look like a piker the way he was tossing dirt.

"Waist deep, so they can get below the flight of any bullets or arrows."

"Gotcha."

Slocum slipped off the high perch and used the wagon for a brace to hold his rifle steady. The hostiles had drawn rein at a good distance, obviously disturbed by the sight of the wagon beds.

"Need us yet?" Summerset asked, sounding out of breath as the four dug the pit. Their shovels rang as more dirt was piled up at both ends.

"Not yet."

Slocum considered the distance. Way past the range of

the .44–40, but he thought if he lobbed a bullet into them and managed to get lucky—it might find a target. He aimed his sights far over the lead one's head. Then shot.

A piebald horse reared with his rider clinging to him and then fell over backward, obviously the victim of his shot. He'd not intended to kill a horse, but his mistake had thrown the Cayuse into a frenzy of war cries. Several rode over, looking at the still rider on the ground. He must have been hurt in the fall. The piebald never got up either.

It worked once. Perhaps he could do some damage again. Then he recalled the dynamite. He set down the rifle and ripped open the side pocket of the saddlebags where he'd stored it. His fist full of the four sticks, he ran for the sage.

"Slocum, where in the hell are you going?" Marley shouted.

"Never mind, keep digging." He set four sticks up in various sites. Each red marker stood in a sagebrush plant, fifty yards from the wagon, about thirty feet apart.

His explosives in place, he ran for cover, as the drum of hooves and the coyote yapping of war cries told him hell was on its way. Out of breath, he slid behind the wagon box for cover.

"Hold your fire. Summerset, see that red stick? Those Indians get close, you open fire on it. Marley, you get the center one. There's one on the left for you, Able. I'll get the second one from the right. Let them get close now," he said to Lenore.

"Keep their heads down and you, too," he shouted at Bird in the trench with the small ones. She answered him with a nod and went out of sight in the pit.

He turned back and heard the wailing charge of the Cayuse as they drove their ponies hell bent for the small fort. All Slocum could think was *Ride, Squaw, ride!*

12

The dust of their charging ponies obscured Slocum's seeing his sticks of explosives. Arrows whizzed by and bullets came like mad hornets, splintering wagon boards and ripping through the air. Their war cries shattered the air as the renegades charged around the makeshift fort. But his men's pistols were answering the attack. Several Indians and a half dozen horses were down.

Slocum jammed fresh ammo in his Winchester. He glanced over and noticed Bird was hugging the two younger ones protectively in the hole. Good. The two boys and the men were taking deliberate shots, and the din outside their ring began to grow less.

"They're going back," Summerset shouted.

"Reload," Slocum said. "They ain't through with us."

The war party ran off to regroup on a broad knoll. Slocum drew a bead on a buck on his hands and knees, crawling away from a fallen horse. The loincloth-clad Cayuse was dragging a rifle with him. The 44–40 cracked in an ear-shattering round and the buck dropped flat. Slocum watched where he went down. He jumped up and ran out to snatch up the new rifle. With a glance at the Cayuse, he made long strides and was back in the fort handing the rifle to Summerset.

"Whew, we've got two now," the man said with pride.

There were a half dozen combatants down; some might

have arms they could use and ammo. He caught sight of Mrs. Marley. A ribbon of hair in her dust-floured face, she pushed fresh rounds in his Winchester's magazine.

"Cover me," Slocum said, anxious to make another dart out there for more, and he set out for the nearest Cayuse on the ground. The man was dead. His eyes glazed open at the high sun. Slocum swept up his pistol and jammed it in his waistband. A few yards beyond, the brass-tack-decorated stock of a repeater lay in the open.

"Slocum, they're coming back!" Lenore shouted. Then she answered the Indians' yipping and shot in the direction of the knoll to fend off the savages. He stuck the Indian's rifle under his arm, and making long strides for his next goal, he saw a new long gun in the hands of downed Cayuse, a short-bodied one who lay on his side behind the body of a bloody paint horse.

Too late, Slocum realized that Indian on the ground was only pretending. He rose to his knees and drew a bead on Slocum's chest. Too late to stop and take evasive actions, Slocum never broke stride. He drew back the rifle with both hands on the barrel and began to swing it for the man's head. The Cayuse's hammer clicked on a dud and the stock struck him beside the head at the same moment. Slocum tore the gun from his grasp. But he knew his nine lives would soon be used up—the Cayuse were coming back for more. The smoke of their shots and loud screaming began to grow.

He had three more weapons. Not looking back, he charged for the wagon boxes and was running full out when he discovered that the buck who once owned the rifle was on his tracks in hot pursuit of him.

A shot rang out from the fort and a bullet struck the bare-chested Indian in the center of his sternum. Over his shoulder Slocum caught a glimpse of him throwing up his arms and then falling backward. By then Slocum was around the wagon, and the thud of bullets forced him to get down.

"How much longer will they attack us?" Lenore asked.

"Long as they feel like it. They're pretty soaked up in alcohol. So bad some can't even stay on their horses." He pointed his barrel toward one who fell off then could hardly run after his horse.

"I noticed."

"Who shot that buck off my tail?"

"Able Marley."

"Thanks, Able," he said, before the screams of the charging Cayuse drowned out their talking.

Gunsmoke blurred his watering eyes and nose. His mouth felt like a parched desert and the mid-morning sun bore down on them. Shots rang out from his defenders and more toll was taken by his shooters. An arrow creased Summerset's arm and Mrs. Marley quickly tied a bandanna around it.

Gun-shy from the first ill-fated attack, the Cayuse stayed farther back this time, which made their bows and arrows less effective. They also acted less enthused than they were the first time, from Slocum's viewpoint. They'd lost several warriors in that first round, and no doubt some were licking their wounds on the knoll.

"You seen a chief?" Slocum shouted at his crew when the Indians again drew back.

"Not one with a headdress," Marley said, raising up to look at the fleeing riders.

"Summerset, can you see that dynamite stick on your side?"

"Yeah, its in that patch of sage."

"Good," Slocum said. "Able, can you see the left one?"

"No, sir."

"I'll go set it up," Slocum said.

"No, I can do it." The boy scrambled to his feet and his brogans flew. Around horse carcasses and fallen Indians, he dove for the sagebrush, set up the stick and flew back.

Slocum could see his stick. It was right in the range that the attackers were coming to.

"You two empty your rifles into those bushes when they get there. Get ready, they've about got their nerve worked up again."

They began to howl and mill around holding bows and rifles over their heads. The dust they stirred about obscured them, but soon they came tearing downhill.

Slocum took aim. "Not too quick."

He heard the drum of driving horses, the hair-raising screams and then the rapid fire of two rifles beside him. The middle stick exploded first, throwing horses and riders in the air; then before the left flank of the chargers could figure out what happened Able's last bullet struck the stick on that side. Warriors and mounts all went up in a great blast of dust and destruction.

"Here." Lenore tossed Slocum her rifle and he caught it, rolled back in position, and the third round found more dynamite. The Cayuse fled to the right at the loud blast; then there was another explosion in their midst and the crowd of milling horses and riders were torn apart.

Dallia Marley stood in the trench holding the smoking shotgun. She'd exploded the last one, and Slocum could see the results as the wind swept the battlefield of dust and gunfire.

The war cries were over. Screams of injured horses filled the air. Crippled ones struggled to rise and stumbled around needing to be put out of their misery. The defenders waited wordlessly for the tan fog to completely clear. Rifles at their cheeks, seconds pounded by like long minutes. Impatience grew like the bitterness of the ash on their tongues. Slocum hoped his plan had been enough. He had no more tricks left. They were low on ammo.

"They're riding away!" Marley shouted.

"Not so fast. They could be laying out there like that rifle tooter that about got me," Slocum said, drawing his Colt. He'd need it to put away the severely injured horses if nothing else.

Toward the knoll rode over a dozen riders, the fight obviously gone from them. The number of dead and injured Cayuse shocked Slocum. Over a dozen more bodies were strewed about the ground. Twice that many horses. He shot a badly injured horse in the forehead and it collapsed.

An Indian on his butt with a broken leg waved at him. "Me no fight."

"Throw your knife away and no tricks."

The Indian obeyed, looking in some pain over his shattered leg. Slocum shot three more moaning horses. Two more bucks raised their hands and surrendered. By then Marley and Able were in the field taking prisoners. Dewayne and his son, Alex, were working the south end of the carnage, destroying injured ponies and rounding up defeated Cayuse.

The eight prisoners were forced to sit on the ground. Slocum gave the guards orders to shoot to kill if they so much as moved an inch. He went back to check on the women and children.

"Bird did fine," Mrs. Marley bragged. "The children say she kept pushing their heads down."

"About pushed us in the ground," the small boy complained.

Slocum gave the dirty-faced Indian girl a nod of approval. "Thanks. Thanks to all of you."

"What do we do now?" Lenore asked.

"Round up the horses we can find, put at least one wagon back up and get to Cross Creek."

"What about the prisoners?"

"Take 'em along. The Army can deal with them."

"I wasn't sure at all how this would turn out when you wanted to stand and fight," Lenore said.

Slocum bobbed his head in deep consideration of the whole thing. He had not been sure either, with women, children and an untried force. But it had worked. He studied the direction the Cayuse had gone toward the hills and shook his head. One more thing niggled him about the afternoon. Among the dead and prisoners, he'd seen no sign of Running Dog or Tall Horse.

"Better find us some horses, get hitched and be quick," he said to his dust- and gray-gunsmoke-floured crew.

13

Darkness replaced twilight before Slocum hailed the guards at the edge of town. He rode bareback in the lead, on a captured Indian pony.

"Friends coming in from the basin," he told the armed men.

"Yeah, we can see that. Have any trouble?"

"Some," Slocum said. "They attacked us. We bit back. There's several dead renegades out there and we took some prisoners."

"You and these women?" The guard looked over the wagons and the line of prisoners in the dim light.

"Hey, there's five men here, too," Slocum said, put out at the man's sarcastic words about his outfit.

"How come ya took prisoners?"

"We aren't savages." Slocum booted the paint pony so that he rode on before he lost any more of his temper.

"Yeah, you're right about that," the guard said behind him.

He was anxious to learn about Squaw. Unusual she hadn't come back to see about them after she warned the sheriff. Even more so the guards didn't seem to know a thing about the fight—they should have if she had made it there.

He dismounted heavily before the jail. A figure came to the door. "That you, Slocum?"

"Yes, and I've got some prisoners," he told the deputy.

"Huh?"

"Cayuse."

"Hell, we just chain them drunk Injuns to the fence."

"No, these need to be put in cells. Anyone seen the Army?"

"Not yet, but the sheriff expects them any day."

"Sure. Did the Cayuse Indian woman report we were being attacked this morning?"

"No, ain't seen her either. Why, were you attacked up there?"

"Something's happened to Squaw, hasn't it?" Summerset asked, herding the downtrodden Cayuse into the jail.

"She never got here?" Slocum looked at the deputy in disappointment.

"I ain't seen hide nor hair of any squaw," the younger man said.

"Bothers me that she never returned with help."

"Help?" the deputy blurted out. "Hell, we knowed you was fighting Injuns out there, we'd've sent a posse. These boys help, too?"

"Those two are men," Slocum said and both boys beamed, standing under the lamplight in the outer office. "Take my word for it. They did their share of shooting all afternoon."

"Ain't been much happened here. Lots of folks coming in, though."

"Good. Bad news is the renegades have already begun killing folks. I found the Bacons slaughtered."

"Bacons?" McGrim asked, hurrying through the doorway. "Saw you took some prisoners?"

"A dozen Cayuse. But that's a drop in the bucket to the war party. And I'd bet good money they're getting their whiskey from Terry."

"He's worthless," McGrim said, looking over the Indians in his cells. "I'll hold them for the Army." He turned back with a disgusted look on his face. "What about the others in the basin?"

Slocum shook his head. "I warned all of them. Cowski's not coming. Bacons were murdered before I got there."

"Any notion where they'll strike next?"

"No, but I'm going back and look for Squaw. She left out there before the attack to warn you. She never made it here."

McGrim cocked a bushy eyebrow. "You reckon they got her?"

"Not for certain, but she either had a big problem or they caught her."

"Mr. Slocum, I want to go along."

He turned and looked at the thin-shouldered, lanky Able Marley, a boy of perhaps sixteen. Then he shook his head— no way he could ever ride back and tell his mother that the Cayuse killed him.

"Pa went to Texas by his self at less than my age."

"That was different." Slocum looked around the room and finally saw the ripe figure of his mother. "Ma'am, tell him—"

"Dallia." She corrected him with her name and shook her head to dismiss his objections. With her long hand, she swept the loose ribbons of hair back from her tired face in a dramatic move that turned all eyes in the silent crowd on her. "He asked me a few minutes ago. He knew what you aimed to do when you got those Injuns in the jail. I said he could go if you trusted him."

"Trusted him?" Slocum frowned at the notion of the whole thing.

"He ain't a boy any longer. Today made all of us a lot older. I said he could go." There was a set in her brown eyes, a determined look. She was backing her son, who ached to complete his test to be a man.

Slocum looked at Marley. The man dropped his gaze without a word; then slow-like he nodded his approval.

"Come on, Able. We need fresh horses," Slocum said, and started for the doorway.

"What about rifles?" McGrim asked. "I can send more help—"

"We've got plenty. Might send along some ammo. Two of us is enough, if we can get her out alive."

"Ammo's coming. Go to the livery and tell Dan you need fresh horses. I'll cover the bill," McGrim said after them.

Her money? It was in his saddlebags on the black horse she rode out on. Those Injuns ever discovered it, they'd sure spend it fast on whiskey and a good time. Damn, he better locate her and quick.

The liveryman, Dan, found them two stout horses and saddles. They were busy saddling them when McGrim brought their ammunition and put a box in each horse's pouches. Summerset stuck new .44–40s in their scabbards.

Lenore brought them both blanket rolls, and Mrs. Marley, Dallia, tied a sack full of jerky and candy from the store to each saddle horn so they wouldn't starve. In less then twenty minutes they were ready to ride.

"Be sure the citizens don't get rope hungry waiting on the Army," Slocum said to McGrim.

"I will. I sure hope they send those troops by tomorrow."

"May take some time for them to get here. Goodbye, everyone," Slocum said, and saluted his friends.

Able held his reins high passing through the crowd and nodded to various individuals, wishing them well. They rode out of Cross Creek in a long trot. All Slocum knew to do was go back and track her from where she'd left them. Maybe he could learn something about her disappearance.

The boy never asked any questions. They rode for an hour through the night, and Slocum reined up on a high point to search for any signs of the Indians. No sense riding right into their camp. Nothing but some coyotes yapping at the quarter moon. He nodded to Able and they rode on.

Past midnight, they reached the attack scene. Slocum went wide of the place, staying close to the timber in case the Cayuse had come back to inter their dead. Saw nothing, so he motioned for the boy to move up in the pines.

"Hobble your horse. We'll catch a little shut-eye here. Tomorrow will be another long one."

"Right." The boy bound off and began loosening his girth. "Leave him saddled?"

"Be best. We might need to run for it."

"Mr. Slocum, all you need do is tell me what I need to do to help you."

"You're doing fine, Able. Just Slocum will do—no mister. And I'm kind of used to doing it myself, so you ask when you need to know anything."

"I will, sir."

"Get some sleep," he said, heading for the edge of the trees to look for any signs.

"You aren't going to sleep?"

"Oh, I will in a few minutes. I want to check around one more time."

"Yes, sir."

He could have saved the trip along the timber—too dark to see anything until he was out in the starlit meadow. Empty-handed was all he got for his time. Perhaps in the morning sunshine he could pick up her trail. He soon was in his blankets and asleep.

Dawn came like a flannel blanket. Birds sang and the magpies were having a feast in the meadow. The notion of the exposed bodies of the dead Cayuse bothered Slocum but he had no time for their burials. He and Able chewed on jerky and rode on the tracks of the black horse he found. She had stayed in the trees most of the way not to expose herself.

An hour later, Slocum discovered other tracks where two riders closed in and no doubt took her prisoner. Best he could read the signs, they led her to the south. *Damn. Squaw, we're coming,* he thought. The two began to push their horses.

"They've got a twenty-four-hour head start. Can we catch them?" Able asked.

"They'll get confident of themselves and den up."

"Never thought of that."

"Don't worry, all the things I can think about might turn up wrong, too." Slocum shared a smile with the youngster and they rode on.

The timber country they crossed over soon opened into a vast, open grassland. Slocum scanned it for any smoke or sign of them. Seeing nothing, they booted their ponies on.

Mid-morning, they watered their horses at a small, marshy trickle.

"Never been in this country before," Able said, looking around.

"Guess it's Indian land."

"Could be. Shame, it would make good range."

Slocum agreed. The tracks told him the kidnappers were traveling at a walk. If they kept up a trot, Slocum hoped to catch up to them before dark.

"Let's ride," he said, and both mounted up.

They discovered a cabin with smoke coming from the chimney. Slocum rode around in the timber observing the place. Rosin boughs brushed their legs as they made a steady circle of the place at a good distance. At last, Slocum reined in his bay and the horse dropped his head to snort in the needles.

"I can't tell if any of the horses in the pen are black or not."

Able shook his head. "I sure can't. Guess there's some in there. Reckon they're in the cabin?" he asked in an awed whisper.

"We better wait till it's dark to ride in there and keep an eye on things."

"What if they aren't there?"

"We'll ride on."

"I understand. But they'll have a bigger gap between us and them?"

"They won't ride forever."

"Guess I'm just anxious."

"Anxious in this business will get you hurt."

"Yes, sir." He dropped off his horse and loosened his girth.

Slocum nodded in approval and did the same. He checked the sun. It would be a few hours' wait until darkness.

No one came out the front door the whole time they waited. Slocum watched the blood red sunset fire the cabin's log walls and then twilight's soft light soon smother the small basin. Strange in this time no one left the log structure. The fire had even gone out. No smoke from the chimney. He nodded to the boy—it was time to cinch up and ride in.

Colt in his hand, they came across the open ground with held breath. No signs of anyone, Slocum dropped from the saddle. The rubber grips of the gun butt in his sweaty hand, he made a sign for the boy to stay back. Able sat in the saddle, a Winchester held in the ready.

Slocum's soles crossed the buckshot ground with only a small shuffle.

"Hello, the house?"

Nothing.

He stepped beside the door and pulled the drawstring. With a loud creak it swung inward, and he waited a few seconds. Nothing. Were the two savages inside? His ear turned to listen for any telltale sound. In one big step, he charged over the threshold and was in the dark room, his gun barrel leveled at anything.

Then, satisfied the cabin's interior contained no threat, he struck a match looking for a lamp. He discovered some candles and stepped across a turned-over chair to light them. He raised the light, casting large shadows of his own on the walls.

"Rider coming," Able said.

Slocum set the candles down and went to the door. Obviously, there had been a struggle inside—who was coming or coming back? He stood in the doorway as the rider approached in the low light.

"Wonder who it is," Able said.

"No telling," Slocum said.

"What's going on here?" the intruder demanded. "Where's my wife?"

The man was medium built and wore a high-crown hat. A mustache covered his upper lip, and even in the growing darkness, Slocum could see he was upset.

"Where the hell is my wife?"

"We're trailing some renegades kidnapped a Cayuse woman to here and thought they might be hiding in this cabin," Slocum explained.

"Hiding in my cabin—you seen Janie?"

"We been up in the trees over there for the past three hours and haven't seen anyone."

"Oh, damn, Janie, Janie." He burst past Slocum and dove through the casing into the room. "Where are you?"

Slocum shared a sobering head shake with Able and then turned back to see what the man had found. He entered the cabin and found the man righting the chair by the table.

"She ain't here," he said like someone in a trance.

"Able, go scout around the place," Slocum said over his shoulder, and the boy agreed, hurrying off.

"Name's Dane Rystrum."

"Slocum's mine. Your wife a homebody?"

"Yes, she tends a small garden out back, sews and cans."

Slocum guessed the man to be in his mid-thirties. Maybe a little older. He showed lots of signs of sun and weather on his face.

"Can't figure where she's gone."

"Rystrum, those two bucks were here. We followed their tracks to this place. I'm not trying to scare you, but they could have taken her."

"No signs of a struggle in here, 'cept that chair was on the floor. That boy of yours looking around outside?"

"Yes, his name's Able and he's my deputy, not my boy."

"You the sheriff?"

"No, just the man working for him."

"Good enough. Ah, I'll go outside and look around, too. You don't think—"

"I don't think anything, except these two are killers. They murdered the Cayuse woman's baby up in Washington about a week ago."

He headed for the doorway, but stopped in his tracks when Able returned holding something.

"Your wife's shawl?" Able asked.

"It is. Where did you find it?"

"At the open garden gate, on the ground."

"Wait," Slocum said. "Let's take a light and see if we can read any tracks."

Armed with the candle reflector, he took the lead around the cabin. Knelt down, he studied the scuff marks and the barefoot pony tracks. The renegades had been there. He handed the light to Rystrum for the man to go search the plot.

"What do you figure?" Able asked under his breath.

"They took his wife and rode on fearing detection. They left those horses in the corral to throw us off, or we were so close they ran off. I'd have never believed they wouldn't take the horses in the pen, though."

"No sign of her. But she'd never lose her shawl," Rystrum announced, coming back to them.

"We can't see in the night. Best put our horses up and get after them at first light," Slocum said.

"But they'll—my wife." Rystrum looked defeated. "I know we couldn't see our hands in front of our faces, let alone dim tracks. Still I want to do something for her."

"All three of us do. We'll track them come first light. Best thing you can do for her now is get some sleep, so you can ride tomorrow."

"Yeah," Rystrum surrendered. "I only left her for a few hours—"

"No one warned you about the renegade uprising?"

"No."

"They tried to tell everyone."

"I understand. Better put your horses in the pen. There's grain in the bin; put a nose bag on them. I'll go see what I can stir up for grub."

"I can handle the horses," Able volunteered.

"Thanks," Slocum said and trailed along with the rancher. "This Indian land?"

"Yeah, Janie's my wife. She's Nez Percé. Why I'm here."

"Most of the troublemakers are Cayuse."

"Figures. They weren't very happy about being thrown in here in the first place with the Nez Percé. Ain't many of the Cayuse left either. Smallpox and cholera killed lots of them before the government set up this reservation."

They had rounded the house and headed for the front door when Rystrum stopped and shook his head. "Sure hope she's all right. She's just a slip of a thing . . ."

Slocum clapped him on the shoulder to reassure the man obviously caught up in his emotions. "We'll find her."

He wiped his nose with the side of his hand and snuffed it. "Damn, I sure hope so."

14

The three men left the cabin at the break of dawn. The tracks of the renegades' barefoot horses still went south. Slocum could find the shoe prints of Squaw's black horse, too. Their trail began to edge westerly by mid-morning. Slocum was grateful for Rystrum's food and coffee though the rancher acted even more edgy about the matter of his wife's disappearance as they rode.

"Won't have left her alone—if I'd figured—"

"Can't lick up spilt milk. We'll run them down," Slocum said to reassure the man.

"I'm thirty-seven. Never been married before. She's, aw hell, maybe fifteen. I tell myself she's older—acts older than some silly white girl, but Slocum, she means more than this ranch or anything to me."

"Been married long?"

"Near two years. Best damn two years in my life. I've been all over the West. Drove cattle to Kansas, Montana, worked for some big outfits. My two-bit outfit ain't much, but without her—I reckon my life will be over if anything's happened to her."

"Never that easy. Life is for the survivors. I hope she's all right, but you'll have to go on otherwise as well."

"Can we hurry along faster?"

"No, I don't want them to know we're coming."

"Good point." He dropped down in the saddle and looked defeated.

Slocum nodded. He wished he knew the land better or they had an Indian guide. So far, the overwrought Rystrum wasn't lots of help for a man who ran cows in this country.

"You can't think of a big spring they might head for, or a river?"

"Why's that?" Rystrum asked.

"They might want to den up and rest."

"Black Beaver Creek."

"Good. How far away?"

"Few miles over those hills."

Slocum looked to the west and nodded. "Good. Let's lope."

Sunlight danced off diamonds on the water's surface. They let their horses drink while Slocum scoured the bank for signs.

"Ride over on the far bank," he said to Able, over the rustle of the stream, "and see if they came out over there."

The youth pushed his horse into the creek, and the water was up to the pony's knees as he splashed across. Able rode up and down in search of tracks where the party had left the water.

"Ain't none," he shouted back to Slocum, who was squatted on his heels waiting for the report.

"All right. You go upstream. I'll ride down, and maybe we can find where they climbed out."

Able gave him a wave and rode his pony northward in the water. Slocum set the stirrup, stepped in it, swung aboard his bay and nodded to Rystrum. "You can ride on the bank and watch for sign."

An hour later, there was still no trace of where they'd ridden out of the water. Slocum put the bay on the bank and dismounted.

"Wonder if the boy found anything—"

Both men turned to the sounds of shots. Panic-driven, Slocum hit the saddle. "Come on. That boy's in trouble."

His horse busting through the brush, Slocum came into a clearing and could see Able riding bent over the saddle and four war-painted bucks hard on his heels, tearing down bushes and small trees. Slocum reached back and drew the .44-40 out of the scabbard, slapped a cartridge in the chamber and pressed the walnut stock to his cheek.

The rifle kicked his shoulder when he fired at the lead buck. Standing in the stirrups, he levered in another shell and snapped off another round that took the second screaming buck off the butt of his pony. The others veered off.

Able slid his horse up on his hind feet, and pale-faced, he turned to look back. "Came out of nowhere," the youth gasped.

"See any camp?"

"I could smell a little smoke. I think there's one upstream."

"We going to charge it?" Rystrum asked, trying to control his excited horse.

"Not if there's umpteen Injuns up there," Slocum said.

"Well, they'll know we're here after you shot two of them."

"You see anything?" Slocum asked the youth.

Looking taken back by the whole incident, he shook his head. "I was"—he swallowed hard—"just riding along when they came running at me screaming and shooting."

"Good thing you can ride like the wind," Slocum said to reassure the youth and went over to look at the downed buck.

Before he knelt down beside the still body, he searched around warily. No sense taking any chances. The rifle over his knee, he reached out and started to roll the Indian over on his back. Like an explosion, the buck came alive with a knife in his hand and screamed. In a split second, Slocum threw up the rifle to ward off the knife attack and drove his knee hard into the Indian's crotch. His swiftness saved him from the cutting edge, and the Indian's face paled. The knife clattered to the ground, and the buck's copper mouth formed an O, moaning in misery. Hands clutching his loincloth, his eyes narrowed.

In his fist, Slocum gathered him up by the front of his shirt. "What's your name?"

"Red Bear."

"I'm looking for two Cayuse—Running Dog and Tall Horse. They in your camp?"

"No—rode on."

"They have two women with them?"

The buck nodded, still holding his privates in obvious discomfort.

"Where did they go?" Rystrum asked.

"Go to Feather Creek."

Slocum turned to the rancher. "You know where that is?"

"Yeah."

"Good. You get your ass back to camp. Soldiers'll be here shortly; they'll teach you a lesson in war parties."

"Soldiers come?" The buck's brown eyes flew wide open.

"Damn right. They'll come beat your ass for making war on us."

"Burn tepees, rape our women, kill us all—"

"That's right. You better go back and tell them the Army's coming soon."

"Me go," the buck said, and half stumbled leaving.

They watched him run away, mumbling and talking to himself.

"Why tell him that?" Able asked.

"That's all they fear. If they're worried enough about the Army coming, they may leave us alone."

"Good idea."

"You know a short cut to this Feather place?" Slocum asked Rystrum.

"I do."

"Good. Let's get there."

When he stepped in the saddle, all he could think about was Squaw and her welfare. *We're coming, girl.*

15

Cooking smoke swirled on the ground in the camp of the Indians set along Feather Creek. Squaws came out of their tepees and stood with their arms crossed over their bosoms to view them. Bashful small children with thumbs in their mouths, wearing only short shirts, hung around the women's leather-fringed skirts. They all looked unwashed, unkempt, their pride swallowed and only the hard looks remaining of a once strong society.

"No dogs in camp," Slocum said to the youth beside him. Both men carried rifles in the cradle of their arms.

"What's that mean?"

"Times're hard. They ate them."

Able nodded, but still acted watchful of everything.

Then an old man with white hair, in a many beaded deer-skin outfit, came out of a lodge and stood as if waiting for them. A few more men carrying older rifles joined him.

"Ho, Chief," Slocum said, holding up his palm in a sign of peace.

"Ho, white man. Why you come my camp?"

"Looking for two women. This man's wife and a Cayuse woman." He motioned with a head toss to Rystrum as they pulled up three abreast.

"You Janie's man?" the chief asked.

"Yes. They took her from my place a day ago," Rystrum said.

The elder made a sour face. "They say she tired living with white men."

Slocum stuck his rifle barrel out in time to stop Rystrum from kicking his horse forward. "Easy, pard. There's only three of us," he said, then turned back to the wizened-faced old man. "Chief, they speak lies. Are they here?"

When the chief shook his head, Slocum knew the pair had ridden on.

"Did both women go with them?" he asked.

"Yes."

"Where did they go?"

He threw his withered dark brown arm toward the south. "Blue Mountains."

"We'll ride on," Slocum said. "These two are liars. They're a disgrace to their people. They killed the Cayuse woman's baby for their own purposes. I saw that. Those women do not travel with them—they're being held as slaves."

"What will you do?" the old man asked.

"Find them," Slocum said. "Let's ride, boys."

Slocum never felt they were on the right tracks after they left the first creek. The pair had switched horses or something. No sign of the shod one's tracks either, which only added to his confusion, but unable to do anything else, they rode in the direction of the mountains.

"Never figured it would take this much to find them," Rystrum said.

Slocum agreed. They had no food, nor were they equipped for a lengthy stay.

"Maybe we can find a store," Able offered as they stood in the stirrups, trotting their horses across the open grassland hemmed in by timber-clad hills.

"We need to find one," Slocum agreed. " 'Cept all my money's in those saddlebags with her."

"Aw, no."

Slocum nodded.

Midday, they spotted a small gathering of buildings and rode in that direction. Perhaps someone had seen the Indians and the two women. Slocum figured he had enough money to buy a few items to get them by. They reined up before the building marked "STORE." Dismounting heavily, the three began to dig out their money. All tossed in, they had less than five dollars.

"Bacon, beans, coffee," Slocum said.

His partners agreed, and he headed inside the store to make the purchases. He passed through the open door and went past the stack of material bolts piled high on a table.

"Howdy, stranger," a short man in a white apron said from behind the counter.

"Ten pounds of beans, a slab of bacon and a few pounds of coffee. You got it already ground?"

"Sure do," the man said and hurried around getting the supplies. "You boys must be heading out, buying commodities like this."

"Looking for two Indian bucks who have two Indian women with them."

The man made a face, then nodded. "They went through here early this morning."

"Which way they headed?"

"East, I guess. Paid me with a spanking new twenty-dollar gold piece. Guess they stole it off'n some poor devil."

"That's them. How much do I owe you?" Slocum felt anxious to be on his way. Four or five hours and they'd catch them. Good. Flush with the excitement of his discovery, he waited impatiently while the man did his math on some butcher paper, rechecked it, then at last looked up and nodded.

"Comes to three-ninety."

Slocum counted him out the money and pocketed the rest of his change. His purchases in a cloth sack, he started for the doorway. At the sight of both Rystrum and Able holding their hands up, he blinked in the bright light on the boardwalk.

"Don't move, Slocum." Someone stepped up behind him and jerked his six-gun free. "You want to die, try something."

"These boys are looking for two women that've been kidnapped. Give them this poke in my right hand."

"Don't try nothing." The bounty man took the sack and handed it to Rystrum.

"Boys, them bucks were here this morning. Don't worry about me. I'm a big boy. Go get those women back. They rode east. Can't be a few hours ahead of you." .

"We can't leave you—" Able looked sick at the notion.

"Ride, goddammit!" Slocum swore.

He read the concern in the youth's eyes. But they obeyed and galloped away. Relieved at their obedience, he felt better. Those two should be a real match for the two Cayuse bucks—have to be, or they'd get away and never be found. Rystrum wanted his wife back, and Able would get Squaw out of that mess. He had to believe that. He turned to his own fate, feeling lucky they were allowed to go on.

"What now?" he asked the pair.

"Going to take you back to Cross Creek. Supposed to be some deputies coming from Kansas to meet us there." Carter was all smiles as he walked around inspecting his prisoner. Dressed in cowboy gear and a tall-crowned dark gray felt hat, he filled the bill of most Texas cowboys. His partner dressed the same—they looked like a couple drovers who'd gotten up there in the Northwest, spent all their money and really wanted to be back in Texas. His reward money might be their ticket home, if they weren't already on the run from some sheriff's warrant in the Lone Star State.

Ward was closemouthed. His only comment was to step to the edge of the boardwalk and spit tobacco out in the dust.

"You reckon he's going to try anything?" he finally asked his associate.

"He'll try anything. Anything," Carter warned and shook his head. "I'll go get a rope. Can't believe he just rode into us."

"Small world," Slocum said, disgusted but hopeful that the other two could handle the Cayuse when they caught up with them.

"Get him tied." Ward spat again and wiped his mouth on his sleeve. "I'll feel a damn sight better."

"I'm bringing the rope," Carter said.

In minutes they had him trussed up and on his horse.

The little store man came out and blinked his weak eyes in the bright sun. One hand up to shade them, he said, "Can't tell who will wander in, can you? That's the man killed all those innocent people in Kansas?"

"Women and children," Carter said to reinforce his story.

"Let's ride," Ward said. " 'Fore his friends come back to help him."

No need arguing. Somewhere between there and Cedar Creek he had to outsmart these two. Would the other two get the Indian women free? Damn, he sure had fallen into a mess. No time for these two, but so far they hadn't found his hide-out gun in his boot. A .30-caliber Colt was the ace up his sleeve—or up his pant leg anyway.

Ward led his horse and they left the place they called Union Town. Carter rode drag, but with Slocum's hands bound and his legs tied to the stirrups, there was not much opportunity for him to make a break for it.

"I told you we'd get another chance," Carter bragged behind him.

"Yeah, you sure did. But he was the last one I expected in that place."

"What if you have the wrong man?" Slocum asked.

"Good try. We've got you. Ain't we, Ward?"

"I think so." The man turned in the saddle and nodded.

"Think so? We've got him right here."

"They won't pay the reward," Slocum said.

"They better pay it."

"How you going to get a Kansas court to pay you a reward clear out here?"

"Shut up. You're spoiling all my daydreaming about the foxy ladies I'm going be screwing with that money." Carter laughed out loud. "How about you, Ward?"

"Going to get me a good saddle to ride first thing."

"Aw, hell, you can always get a saddle any old day. We're going out and screw every—"

"I see 'em, too," Ward said to his partner, pointing off across the open country at dust billowing up.

"Indians."

"They still on the warpath?" Ward asked with an edgy voice.

"Why I came to Union Town in the first place, to get away from them," Slocum said, knowing it was no war party. Too much dust—that meant lots of travois with women and children. They never fought with them along, only defended them. But what those two Texans didn't know wouldn't hurt them.

"Come on, we better ride," Carter said, and they headed for the timber.

Slocum rocked in the saddle as they drove their horses into the cover of the trees. From there, the pair peered like mice on the lookout for a tomcat, and so they remained until dark. Too afraid to build a fire, they ate some jerky and never offered Slocum a thing. Then by starlight they headed for Cross Creek.

After getting lost twice, they finally managed to get back on the road. At dawn, they rode past the guards at the edge of town.

"Who've you got there?" the sentry asked.

"A Kansas killer," Carter said and motioned them on.

"Ain't he the guy saved all those folks in the basin?"

"Maybe, but he's wanted in Kansas for murder," Carter said over his shoulder, hurrying them for the jail.

The deputy frowned at the handbill they gave him. "Why, that could be anyone."

"Lock him up," Carter demanded. "It's him."

"What've you got to say about this?" the deputy asked Slocum, getting out his pocketknife.

Carter stuck his hand out and stopped him. "This sumbitch is a killer. Untie him back there."

"Listen, you may be the damn bounty hunter, but I'm the law here. I'll cut him loose wherever I want. Now clear out."

"No way! That sumbitch is worth five hundred dollars to us, and the only way we can collect it is to turn him over to them Kansas deputies coming after him."

"What if the governor won't let them have him?"

"Huh?" Carter asked and frowned at his sleepy-eyed partner.

"It's called extradition," the deputy said, at last cutting through the rope so Slocum was free and could rub his burning wrists. "Them jayhawkers are going to have to talk to the governor before they get him."

"Slocum, Slocum?" Mrs. Marley, Dallia, came through the doorway. Her voluptuous body in the blue dress swung in with her.

"What about my son, Able?" she asked, concerned.

"He's fine. In the company of a good man. They went on after the Indian women when these two showed up." He motioned to the bounty hunters.

"They've got more than her now?" She shook her head as if confused.

"Yes, a man called Rystrum. They took his Indian wife, too."

Worry lines creased her smooth forehead. "What will they do?"

"I'm sure they have the women back by now and should show up here shortly."

She nodded and thanked him, looking somewhat relieved. "Deputy, after all he's done for this community, I can't believe you are even considering putting him back there with those heathen redskins."

The deputy's face turned red and he swallowed hard. "Ma'am, I've got to till Sheriff McGrim gets back, ma'am."

"Well, when he does I am certain he will throw these two scalawags out on their ears as well as release Slocum."

"Yes, ma'am." To Slocum he said, "You can sit back there in the hallway. I'll lock the outer door. All them cells are full of them stinking Injuns."

He nodded he understood as the man picked up a bench for him and carried it through the outer doors of the cell block. Slocum turned and studied the pair of bounty hunters.

"Don't get no ideas about escaping either." Carter waved his finger at him. " 'Cause one of us is staying here around the clock till them Kansas deputies get here."

"Guess you've got company," he said to the deputy, who took a peeved look out in the office then shook his head.

"McGrim'll handle them. I can't. Need my job."

"No problem. Sorry I caused you one."

"Mister, you saved more lives than I can imagine. Folks ain't going to forget all you done for them, regardless what them Kansans think."

Slocum sat down on the bench and the deputy went out, closing the outer door after himself. One look over the dark-eyed prisoners told him the Army still had not come to Cross Creek. Maybe that was where McGrim was at the moment—trying to get them. There would be many more lives lost if they didn't get there shortly. Their presence alone would send most of the renegades packing for home.

Damn, he sure hoped that Able and Rystrum had gotten the Indian women freed. He stretched out on the bench and stared at the flyspecked ceiling. Better wait to try his break-out until later; they might free him anyway before it was all over.

16

Slocum sat at the table in the outer room of the sheriff's office and feasted on fried chicken, mashed potatoes, green beans and fresh biscuits with sweet cream butter. Seated in a chair beside the open door, hugging a Winchester to his chest with a hangdog look written on his sour face, was Ward. Slocum held up the brown crusted drumstick and, before he bit into it, spoke to the bounty hunter. "Remember that jerky you and Carter ate that day you arrested me?"

"Yeah. What about it?"

"I'm going to extend the same courtesy that you and him showed me then. Deputy Jarvis, would you like another piece of fried chicken?"

"Can't say as I wouldn't." The big-framed night shift deputy swung out of his chair before the desk, came over with a white towel for a bib and accepted two pieces with a nod. "Glad I never denied you no damn jerky. You're kinda vindictive about it." Then the lawman laughed aloud.

"Kinda," Slocum agreed, thinking about Dallia's ample body under the dress when she delivered his dinner. That Marley was a lucky man—Slocum hoped he realized his good fortune.

"What's this Kansas business all about?" Jarvis asked.

"An old score. A kid tried to outdraw me one night. He was drunk. I tried to convince him he had no business messing with me—so in the end, I busted him over the head, put him in the alley. He came back a half hour later with his gun ready, burst inside and fired a shot past my ear. I dropped him."

Jarvis nodded. "So self-defense?"

"Not when he was a rich man's son who could buy the judge and jury off."

Holding the white chicken bone in his hand, Jarvis gave him a thoughtful bob of his head. "I see."

"Don't matter," Ward said. He rose and stuck his head out the office door to spit. Then he stepped back and sat on the chair. "They still want you for murder in Kansas."

"Good chicken," Slocum said to Jarvis, as if the other man had never said a word.

"That Mrs. Marley is a remarkable woman," Jarvis agreed. He leaned back in the chair considering his last piece of bird, and smiled. "She ever need any help, I'd sure be there."

"Her son Able's a good hand, too."

"Figure he—"

"Slocum!" Squaw shouted and burst into the room. She rushed over to hug him and Ward jumped to his feet, leveled the rifle. Able came through the doorway next. He saw the rifle, drew out his Colt and busted the bounty hunter over the head. The rifle went off into the floor and, besides making everyone deaf, filled the room with gunsmoke. Ward crumpled to his knees and then fell flat out on his face.

Jarvis came up with a six-gun in his hand and tried to survey everything around him.

"Sumbitch went for his gun was all I saw," Able said, holstering his handgun and picking up the rifle. "Mister, you're plumb dangerous with this thing."

Ward held the top of his head with both hands. "Give me that damn gun."

Able shook his head.

"Get outside, Ward." Jarvis waved him out with his six-shooter. "From here on you're guarding this jail from out there."

"What about my rifle?"

"Evidence. The sheriff may charge you for discharging a firearm in here."

"I've got rights."

"If you don't get the hell out of here, I'm locking you up with them Cayuse in the back. Now get out." Then he dropped his voice. "Aw hell, that gunshot will bring the whole town down here. Cripes sake."

Slocum could hear them already gathering out on the porch and asking what was wrong.

"How did it go, Able?" he asked the youth.

"Running Dog and Tall Horse got away." He dropped his gaze to the floor. "Damned slick. We—me and Rystrum— was worried about them women and decided we better ride on back here."

"You did good."

"She tells me the two of you have a mustang outfit up in Washington."

"Yes."

"That you got some horses branded and pens."

"Tough way to make a living."

"Hey, farming ain't easy."

Slocum nodded.

"You wouldn't mind if I trailed along and learned something about mustanging?"

"Her deal." Slocum motioned to Squaw.

"We talked some about it. She said you had to say it would be all right."

Slocum looked at her and she nodded in approval. Then he turned back to Able. "What's your ma going to say?"

"That I'm old enough to decide things for myself."

"Don't your father need you?"

"We've got things going out there, if they ain't burned us out."

"Well, there's a matter of folks talking about a man and a squaw in camp."

"Don't bother me none."

Slocum listened to Jarvis out in front talking to the crowd and assuring them it was all safe in the jail, only an accidental shot fired that wouldn't happen again. Man, how did you tell a boy of sixteen this might not be what he wanted to do the rest of his life? Squaw's welfare made up the rest of his concern—if the boy stayed long, he needed to make a commitment to her.

"You look at him?" he asked her.

She smiled and nodded in approval.

"Hey, she says you're okay. Fine with me. But I may be detained awhile, so you two work it out. You can have my share of the ones we branded for starters."

Squaw and him both looked pleased. She came over and quietly asked, "You need us get you out of here?"

"No, you two go on and mustang. I'll be out of here shortly."

"Thanks. Come on, Nomie," Able said. "I want you to meet my folks."

"Be there," she said and gazed up at Slocum. "Got good eyes. I look in them."

Slocum nodded slightly. "You be careful. Those two will be back."

"Yes, watch all the time," she said and ran off in a swirl of leather fringe to the doorway, where she stopped and turned back to look at him. "You come help. We get big herd."

"I will." Slocum sat down and buttered a cold biscuit. He took small bites. Dallia would know when she saw them together and heard them talk to each other. An idealistic boy going off with an Indian woman to chase mustangs, live in a ten-by tent—winter and summer. His father would feel cheated losing a farmhand—but his mother would wonder deep in her heart if she could hug her half-breed grand babies when they came by her place. *You can, Dallia,* he thought. You will.

McGrim arrived at sunup and woke Slocum. "You're free on your bail."

"Where's the Army?"

"The fort."

"They going to let the damn renegades run all over everyone? Kill some more families?"

"I'm so mad, Slocum. Government red tape. Some official

from the Indian Agency is coming down to talk to them. Can you imagine that?"

"They won't fear him. All they fear are cannons and uniforms."

"Would you lead a posse against them?" McGrim asked, dropping heavily in his chair.

"Me?" Slocum about laughed. "I'm under arrest."

"Not now. I guarantee—you lead this posse and they won't ever spring you from Oregon, even with that moldy warrant they speak about."

"Ain't it kind of the sheriff's job to lead one."

"Yes, but you can get more out of men than I can. The wagon fight showed it out here in the basin—no one hardly scratched and several Cayuse in the happy hunting grounds. What do you say?"

"Go get Cowski and his dynamite. Have him meet us. We'll need that. Tell everyone to have five days' rations in their saddlebags. Blankets, some horse feed, guns and ammo. Find some scout or tracker knows that country."

"Gentleman Jim Barlow."

Slocum frowned at the lawman's choice. He'd never heard of the man.

"An old coot thinks he's a mountain man. He'll be good enough. What else?"

"A hotel room to sleep in tonight, a bottle of good whiskey and wake me thirty minutes before dawn."

"You're cheap enough."

"Sheriff, sheriff." Carter broke in the room looking all around wild-eyed. "You can't turn him loose."

"He ain't going anywhere. You get off his case. I'll guarantee his appearance in court when Judge Raines gets here and hears this matter."

"Judge Raines? Who in the hell is he?"

"The judge for the eastern district of Oregon."

"When's he coming here?"

"Before the snow flies usually, unless he has a big caseload. Then it'll be later."

Carter stood with his jaw slack. "But those Kansas deputies—"

"We can't let him go unless the judge orders it. That's Oregon law."

"Then I'll take him to the judge—" Carter said.

"No." McGrim shook his head. "Court has to be held in this county 'cause you turned him in in this county."

"He ain't getting off. I'm collecting that damn reward."

"Listen." McGrim caught him by the sleeve and whirled him around. "You so much as even threaten him, I'm locking the pair of you up for obstructing justice."

"You can't—"

"Try me and you'll be doing hard time."

Carter backed away. He staggered like a man hit over the head—then he was gone out the door. McGrim gave his disappearance an angry look before he spoke, "Room, whiskey, coming up."

McGrim headed Slocum out the front door into the night. The dark street looked deserted, save for the parked wagons that folks had driven in. Several were camped close by their rigs, bedrolls and blankets spread out on their ground.

They passed a woman sitting up rocking a crying baby. She smiled at them and nodded in the light coming from the saloon across the street.

"Told the bars they could stay open, but no loud music and no cussing," McGrim said as they rounded a rig, stepped over the tongue and went up the steps to the hotel's front door. "Been working all right. So far."

"Where we going to meet in the morning?" Slocum asked.

"Livery."

"Bring me a handgun."

"Oh yeah, plumb forgot that. I do want to thank you for helping us. I know these renegades ain't no skin off your nose."

"Hey, I'm glad, too, that I'm sleeping up here tonight and not on that bench."

"You ever think about staying in Oregon? This country could use more men like you."

They stood before the desk, and the night clerk, looking sleepy-eyed, yawned and stretched his arms over his head. "Evening."

"In need of that room you saved," McGrim said.

"Yes, sir, Sheriff. Room twenty-two. Head of the stairs, go right." He handed McGrim the key.

"I kept one room open, in case," McGrim explained. "Place's booked full otherwise, with all these folks in town."

"Wake me up at four-thirty," Slocum told the clerk, who nodded that he heard him.

"Need anything, holler, my deputy will come on the run. I'm going home and get a little shut eye."

Slocum parted with McGrim and climbed the stairs. Be nice to have a hot bath and shave. Be nice to have lots of things. Every muscle in his back ached, and a small headache was centered in his forehead—even out of jail, he did not feel completely free. If he was real smart, he'd take a horse and ride out, forget the Indian deal. But chances were Carter and Ward were both up, patrolling the streets, ready to recapture him and scurry him out of Oregon and across the line for the reward.

He reached the second floor and turned in the dimly lighted hall. Small candle lamps on the wall shed a dull orange glow on the patterned wallpaper. He stuck the skeleton key in the hole under the knob and clicked it open. Then he turned at a soft rustling noise on the gritty wood floor.

The familiar-looking woman in a robe motioned for him to go inside. He obeyed and she quietly followed him into the dark, stuffy room. She closed the door and put her back to it.

"They let you out?" Dallia asked in a soft whisper.

"Yes."

"Good." Her arms reached out and hugged him tight to her. Their mouths met and he really wished he'd had that hot bath.

"I'm shameless," she hissed when their lips came apart. "I dreamed of that since the first day you rode up. When I started back to the room and saw you, I couldn't help myself."

"Will you be missed?" His hands were on her hips and his butt wanted to push him through her.

"We have a few minutes." She threw her head back and cleared the hair from her eyes.

"You're sure?" He looked into her shadowy eyes and pouty lips. Damn, like a ripe peach, she needed to be plucked.

"I was married at fifteen, had Able nine months later. I've never done anything like this before and still can't imagine why. . . ."

He kissed her and undid the tie to her robe. Their mouths were so on fire, the heat drove out all his senses, but one— take her. He undid the tiny buttons on the front of her flannel nightgown and soon his palm weighted one of her long, firm breasts. His touch drew a gasp from her. With the ball of his thumb he rubbed her nipple until it became engorged. Then he pushed both garments off her shoulders and she stood in the buff before him. The sight of her body even in the dim light took his breath away.

Mouth sealed tight to hers, he toed off his boots. With frantic fingers she undid his belt and pants. They fell on his feet. Then she undid his underwear buttons. His heart stopped when he felt the small callouses on her long hand slip inside and gently coax his dick to life.

He stepped back and stripped off the one-piece suit. Then they rushed to the bed. She sat on the high edge and he came up between her knees. With her butt on the edge, he eased his throbbing glans into her wet gates. His bare soles planted on the gritty floor, he began to pump his way inside. The long white stems of her legs wrapped around him; his butt ached to be at the bottom of her trap.

Their breathing increased; the flames in them grew hotter and higher. Openmouthed, she moaned and tossed her head on the bed. He put even more fury into his part when the walls of her vagina expanded with desire and enclosed his painfully swollen erection. Then deep in his testicles he felt the explosion start up the gun barrel. It flew upward and then, in a blinding blast, shot out the tender end of his sword into her. She went limp and her legs crumpled away from him.

He could see how drunk she looked in the light coming in the grimy window. Shaken, she pushed up on her elbows and shook her head in dismay. Hair streamed down in her face and half hid the smile in the corners of her mouth. She sat up and moved aside the errant hair from her face with her hands. Fascinated, he watched her long breasts crash together. Damn, what a woman.

She scooted her butt off the bed to put one foot on the floor. Then she stepped off and ran a palm down his beard-stubbled face. "I won't forget you."

"Might be better that you did." He watched her move toward the door in the pearl light.

One-handed, she swept up her clothing and tossed it on the end of the bed. Then, hands on her hips, she gave a small laugh. "A farmer's wife has got to have something happen to her that's her own secret. Something so when the children, work and chores have you worn clean to the bone, you can kind of go off in your own head and survive another crisis."

He watched her dress quickly in the flannel nightgown. When he wet his lips, the taste of her remained. He remember the soft touch of the cloth and the feeling of her body's warmth still in the material. The robe on, she nodded.

"Look and be sure the hall's clear?" she asked.

He nodded, realizing that he stood naked with beads of sweat running down the hair on his chest. With a slow twist, he opened the latch, drew the door back and cautiously stuck his head out to see. No one.

"Clear," he said and she stole a quick kiss in passing.

"Take good care of him." Her gaze dropped down to his privates. "He really is nice." And she was gone.

He stood behind the cracked door and listened to her soles on the wood floor, then heard a knob click softly and a door close. With his own door shut at last, he rested with his back to the wall and looked at the tin squares in the ceiling. Damn good thing he didn't ride off. Whew. Even his headache was gone when he crossed the room and opened the window to let some of the room's heat out. A rush of cool air swept over his bare skin when he straightened. The faint flavor of violet in his nose and on his tongue, he luxuriated dreamlike in the recall of their fast ride down the river of passion.

Damn, four-thirty would come early.

17

Slocum accepted the steaming cup of coffee from Lenore. The straight-backed ranch woman wore a calico dress that emphasized her slender, willowy form. Hair up in a bun behind her head, she stayed beside him in the darkness outside the livery as if looking out for his interest.

"They're getting you a plate of breakfast," she said.

Still not completely awake, he nodded and considered the steam coming from the metal cup's contents. "Thanks. You seen McGrim around?"

He searched over the crowd of men who were standing as a group and eating from the food served by the various women.

"I think he went back to the office for more guns and ammo," she said, taking a heaping plate from a large woman and thanking her. When she turned to face him with his food, she offered to hold his coffee so he might eat.

"Let's go over by that wagon wheel. My coffee can sit there and that will free you."

"I'm free now," she said.

He glanced at her. Those words meant more than that she had no obligations with the crew tending the fires and cooking.

"Oh, we have everything cooked and there's plenty of women to serve."

"Well, I appreciate your company."

"No, we all owe you. I was so scared up at the wagon fight, but if you had not done what you did and we'd run, they would have swooped down and gotten us all."

"Got lucky. They were poor shots with those new rifles."

"Perhaps. Still you had the forethought to do it right."

He considered the heaping plate of food—scrambled eggs, browned meat, biscuits smothering in flour gravy. The thoughts of it filled his mouth with saliva.

"Tell me about Lenore," he said, taking the fork and looking into her deep blue eyes.

"What is there to tell? I'm an old maid who takes care of her brother and his son like a wife they should have already chosen." She folded her arms and looked away.

"No man in your life?"

She gave a soft laugh. "No one serious since I was sixteen."

Slocum chewed on the first mouthful and nodded. "Maybe you've got the threshold too high."

She cut a sharp look aside at him and then turned back. "I don't want someone I have to nursemaid."

The flavor of the smoked side meat and the eggs blended together in a tasty bit. He wondered about her. She'd come to stake a claim on him. Of course, that would not work—no way, even if he was cleared of Carter and Ward, that he could remain in this land. In the cool predawn air, masticating his food in pleasure-filled forkfuls, he had no answer for her.

"One day, he'll come riding up to your front door and you'll know."

"I did this week when you came."

"Sorry, but I've got more crosses to bear than those two bounty hunters." He dropped his attention back to his plate. "No matter how this Indian business turns out, I'll have to ride on when it's over."

"McGrim said the judge would never let them take you."

"Good man."

"He comes to my chin." She frowned at him.

"So?"

She closed her eyes and then shook her head. "Are all tall men like you?"

"Me?"

"Yes, I've never met one wasn't taken or else he's a damn sugar foot. Your kind must have your heads in the clouds."

He smiled at the sharp edge in her voice. Someone was leading a horse toward him. In haste, he downed the coffee and spotted the gunbelt hanging on the horn. Handing her the plate and cup, he smiled. "Better reconsider the man. He's long on good sense and he won't forget you. Damn sure won't take any nursemaiding."

"You playing cupid?" She made a displeased face for his benefit.

"Dan says this is his best horse," the youth announced.

"Good. Thank him," he said, taking the reins. Then he unhooked the gunbelt off the horn. She took the leather lines and he undid the buckle, strapping the holster set on his waist. With his right hand, he drew the Colt, checked the cylinders and, satisfied it was loaded, put it away.

"I came here to talk you into coming by when this was over."

He nodded that he understood her purpose.

"Took lots of nerve for me to do this."

"I know it did. I'm sorry. It can't work for us."

She pursed her thin lips tight, then chewed on the bottom one. "Guess the things you want the most in this world you can't have."

He tightened the cinch and nodded. "Guess you sized it about right. Think about the sheriff. He's a good man."

"Slocum, I hope you find that place you're looking for. After all you've done here, you damn sure deserve it. Better get to dish washing." She strode off with his dirty dishes.

"She been talking to you?" McGrim asked, riding up and looking after her.

"Brought me breakfast is all."

"If I didn't figure she'd give me the cold shoulder, I'd go up there and see her after this is over." McGrim sat his horse and squeezed the saddle horn with both hands.

His foot in the stirrup, Slocum swung up. "You might ought to do that. You could do worse."

"Reckon she's as cold as she acts?"

Slocum shook his head to dismiss the man's concern. "I doubt it."

"We better ride," McGrim said. "Boys, all of you get ready to mount up—where we going, Slocum?"

"We'll check the basin first."

McGrim nodded his approval. "Got over fifty men, armed and all on good horses. Town's covered, too. There's forty men left, plus many of the women who say they can shoot."

"Good," Slocum said, and they left the crowded street of waving women and children for the road west.

"Gentleman Jim's meeting us out here at the bridge," McGrim told him as they rode.

When they drew close enough, Slocum saw the roman-nosed gray horse standing in the road and a bearded man wearing a buffalo vest sitting on him, balancing a Sharps rifle on his knee. The wide-brimmed sombrero shaded his face, but his mouth made a hole in the thick facial hair when he spoke in a gravelly voice, "Slocum, they call you. Morning, McGrim." He bobbed his head toward the sheriff in greeting.

"Good to meet you, Jim. Seen any sign of the renegades?"

"They're still up here. I seen a big fire reflecting off the clouds up near the Terry place."

"Good, maybe they'll be too hungover to fight," Slocum said as the guide and his gray fell in with them.

"Doubt that serious. They been making raids. I doubt there's a place left up here they ain't raided. Course with the folks gone, ain't a bit hard to raid a place."

"Those folks needed to be in town," McGrim defended his plan.

"They do, but them folks'll all be sick when they do go home. Why, they've stolen every chicken, milk cow, sheep and goat in this basin to feed their dirty-assed crew."

"Can we get into the Terry place and not be discovered?" Slocum asked.

"They ain't real sharp about having out sentries, but this many men's dust boiling up will tell them something's going on."

"What do you recommend?" Slocum asked the scout.

"Ride right up the basin, like you're heading through it. Make camp and lots of smoke. Might stop over at the Summerset place. Come dark, saddle up and ride over there to get in place for a sunup raid."

"You can lead the way in there at night?"

He bobbed his big sombrero in agreement. "Might have to go the last few miles afoot to not alert them."

"Good plan, ain't it, McGrim?"

"I'd say so. What about Cowski?"

"I'll personally go up and invite him to the party," Slocum said. "Now I want to ride back in the line and tell Dewayne Summerset that we'll put up at his place tonight."

"Good idea. Hope they ain't burned his place down."

"Me, too."

He found Dewayne halfway back in the column and invited him to ride up front. Slocum told the man their plans as they rode forward, and he agreed it should work.

"I'm going after Cowski and his dynamite," Slocum explained. "I think we can give those renegades a bellyful of firepower with it."

"Yeah, I hadn't talked to you since all the trouble, but me and my son will sure go to bat for you, if you need us. They ain't taking you out of Oregon."

"I appreciate that, but right now we've got Indians to worry about."

"I understand. Be careful going up there to Cowski's. Could be some small parties riding around, you know?"

"I'll be on the watch." Slocum waved at the man and rode away from the column. He short loped the big chestnut horse. There had been times he'd have given his soul in hell for such a great mount. By mid-morning, he was close to the rancher place and reined the sweaty horse down to a long walk. When he twisted in the saddle, he could make out traces of the posse's dust in the sky.

"Hello the house!"

"That you, Slocum?"

"Yes, still got my hair. How's your's?"

"They only came by once and I let off a stick or two."

Cowski came out of the cabin, shoved the big Texas hat on the back of his head and laughed.

"The Army can't come, so McGrim has a posse of fifty men. We're camping the night at Summerset's place. Then after dark we're going to sneak over to Terry's, which looks to be their headquarters, and have a surprise breakfast for them."

"Good plan. What do you need?"

"You and your dynamite to even the odds."

The rancher scratched his sideburns and studied his dusty boot toes in deep concentration. At last, he looked up and Slocum saw a sparkle in his eyes.

"I'd just join that party. Sounds like a barrel of fun."

Both men laughed out loud.

"Come on in. I've got a new pot of coffee and ain't no use in wasting it by riding off and leaving it on the stove."

Slocum looked down the basin. Still traces of dust in the air. He hoped that the plan worked. One thing, the bowlegged rancher and his explosives would make it even better.

18

A coyote yipped and the soft shuffle of horse hooves filled the night. Slocum and McGrim had both ridden up and down the column to make certain any ringing or metallic sound was muted. All voices were in low whispers, and aside from an occasional horse's snort, the parade remained low key.

Ahead, Jim waited in the canyon where they would leave their animals. Slocum counted on the scout to be certain the way was clear. No moon yet and the starlight was muted by passing clouds. No threat of rain, but Slocum knew everything depended on their secret invasion being in place when daylight lightened the sky over their shoulders.

Past midnight they reached the scout. Ropes were strung tree to tree and the horses hitched. Slocum, McGrim and Jim squatted in a circle, and Slocum and the sheriff listened to the old man.

"Most of them are in camp, best I can tell. They musta gotten a fresh batch of moonshine tonight. You could turn your ear up till the last hour and hear them howling."

"That's good. Hungover you can't fight real good," Slocum said, pleased the plan had gone so smoothly this far. "We need to unload the box of dynamite that Cowski brought and pack it over there to help him get ready."

"I'll get some men to do that," McGrim said.

Thirty minutes later, the scout led the way. Two by two to help each other over the steep hill, the posse began to move out. Slocum and McGrim were in the lead group. Summerset was in charge of making them be quiet and explaining the plan for them to spread out when they reached the others on the far side.

"Thirty-second fuses," Cowski said, showing Slocum the already fused sticks. "Light them, throw 'em and duck."

Slocum agreed. He took the half-full sack from him and slung it over his shoulder. The way uphill proved steep. Around rock outcroppings and large trees they made their way skyward, not pressing themselves, and taking breathers every fifty yards. They were remarkably quiet, which impressed Slocum. Better yet, it would help keep their surprise intact.

An hour later, except for one man falling, coming downhill and hurting his leg, they were all in place. McGrim found some whiskey to ease the man's pain.

The camp dogs barked, but Jim had told them earlier not to worry—they did that over anything and it was not liable to wake up their masters. Minutes crawled by like hours. In the silver light, Slocum could see the many lodges thrown up on the canyon floor.

Bucks began to stir. Dark figures came out to empty their bladders. He and McGrim slipped along the line, telling everyone in place to wait, hold their fire until they gave the command.

Slocum's eyes burned like holes in the hot sand. He needed sleep but was riding the adrenaline in his system. He knew he must be aware when hell broke loose.

"I'm going down and block their going out the canyon."

"Good," McGrim agreed, then he shook his head like something else was bothering him. "You know when Lenore goes back home in a few days and sees it, she's sure going to be upset with what this bunch of renegades did to her house."

"Might make a place for you to get in with her."

"You think so?"

Slocum nodded and left. He hurried through the timber, moving to the left and hoping to be in place when enough daylight struck the camp that he wouldn't miss any of the renegades trying to escape.

He reached the base of the hill and crouched beside a big tree for cover. At the sounds of pounding hooves, he turned his ear and listened to the horses coming. The nighthawks were bringing in the pony herd past his spot. Good, they would only add to the confusion.

If Cowski on the other end of the camp let off enough charges, they should contain the renegades. Wild horses and startled Indians should make a good mix. The light grew stronger. He felt for the matches in his vest pocket. Then he saw the first flare and struck his own match. The fuse on the dynamite stick soon began to fizz with sparkling fire. He reared back and tossed it end over end toward the lodges.

The first blast shattered the air. Horses screamed in sheer panic. Then his charge went off. The frightened horse herd milled about camp, turning over tepees and running down lodges. Men screamed and the morning was split apart by rifles pouring lead into the renegade camp.

Slocum lit fuse after fuse. Each time, he tossed the wax sticks with all of his might into the boiling dust, smoke and utter confusion. The resulting explosions on both ends of the camp left the renegades no place to go but run into the open where the posse could shoot them down.

A white flag soon rose, and Slocum cupped his hands to shout, "Hold your fire!" Twice more he did the same, and finally with McGrim cussing at them to quit their shooting, it trailed off.

Out of the smoke and dust, the bucks came with their hands high. Fear-filled ponies broke past Slocum where he stood with his six-gun in hand, lest any stray buck tried to escape. Shouting posse members, with their rifles ready, came downhill on their boot heels, anxious to collect up the prisoners. Satisfied that the bulk of the spooked horses were by him, Slocum started for the camp.

Those Indians able to stand looked wild-eyed at him, expecting no doubt to be shot on the spot. Several wounded ones moaned on the ground.

"Who speaks English?" he demanded.

A younger one nodded.

"Where is the chief?"

"Big Elk." He pointed to a tall Indian.

"He speak English?"

"Some."

"Where's Terry?"

The boy shrugged.

"Where is the white man made the whiskey?"

"No know."

"What did you find out?" McGrim asked, out of breath from his descent.

"Big Elk, the one with eagle feathers in his hair, over there, is the chief. Terry must not be here. There's no mention of Wolf, who was the chief."

"Disarm them and sit them on the ground out there." McGrim pointed to the grassland to the north. "Shoot anyone who tries to get away."

The posse members heard him and began to push the able-bodied ones out of the smoke of the burning lodges. Slocum and McGrim inspected the camp and then Terry's cabin. No sign of the whiskey trader.

Jarvis brought the sheriff a count. "Three dead, two more won't make it. The other ten or so wounded are only scratched. Plus, counting boys, there are thirty-one sitting on their butts."

"Good job. Get a crew and gather up all these new rifles and ammo, and burn the food supplies, lodges, tepees. Then we need to round up the horse herd and shoot them. Make them renegades think twice before they go off on the warpath again."

"Shoot the horses, sir?" The deputy looked taken back.

"Yes, it's harsh, but it's the only way they'll learn." McGrim looked over at Slocum.

He agreed. "Tough job, but I'll stay and help if you need me."

"No." Jarvis made a great exhale. "If it takes killing the horses to stop the killing of innocent people, I'll get some of the men and we will do it after you all leave."

"Make some stretchers." McGrim told him. "They can

carry their own wounded to Cross Creek. Any of our men get hurt?"

"Charlie Avery. Guess he fell coming off the hill and broke his leg."

"A barber has no business being out here in a posse." McGrim shook his head.

"Hell, he'll be talking about today when all of us are old and gray." Jarvis laughed aloud. "We'll carry him on a stretcher between two horses. He'll be the returning hero of the dynamite war."

"Where's Cowski?" Slocum asked.

The bowlegged rancher came hobbling down through camp, carrying a large feathered war bonnet and a big drum. "Souvenirs, got to have some. Say, Slocum, you ain't a bad hand at tossing that stuff. Thought you might even hit me with one."

"You never saw Terry riding out of here, did you?" McGrim asked.

"No, I'd've dropped that whiskey trader in his tracks, he'd come my way. He gone?"

Slocum nodded. He was about to dread the walk back over the mountain for his horse, when several riders came around leading the whole herd up the canyon.

"I asked them boys to do that," McGrim said.

"Good idea. Any notion where Terry went?" Slocum asked.

"If I did, I'd go look for him myself. He might be hanging out up there by the Snake ferry. I haven't got any authority over there. Have to file with Washington officials and then . . ."

"You mind if I go look for him?"

"No, guess a citizen wouldn't need to obey any state lines to bring him back to Oregon."

Slocum smiled. He checked the Winchester in his scabbard, and McGrim showed him a fresh box of cartridges, then put them in his saddlebag.

"Be careful. Those two Cayuse are still on the loose and Terry won't come back easy."

"I may not come back. I don't find him, I may ride on."

McGrim set his mouth in a tight line, then he bobbed his head. "I'd understand that. But you didn't have to tell me that."

"You've been fair to me. I wanted to be sure you understood my part."

"Ride careful. You've done this country around here a big favor. Folks won't forget you either."

The two shook hands.

"You reckon I should go see Lenore now?" McGrim asked him privately.

"You better," Slocum said and bounded into the saddle. "Good luck with her, my friend."

He wondered about the two bounty hunters, Carter and Ward, as he short loped the bay northward. McGrim never let them ride in the posse. A fact that made him grateful, but late that afternoon when the men and prisoners reached Cross Creek, the pair would be fired up to discover he was gone again. Too bad and too sad.

19

A boy was operating the ferry the evening when Slocum rode up. He led the chestnut horse on the deck and paid him.

"Where's the old man?" he asked, looking around for him.

"On his honeymoon." The boy grinned big. "That old fart up and married a young woman with kids. Guess he's gonna start another family."

"You his boy?"

"Nope, his grandson. I never figured why he wanted one, but he's got her. Won't be back for a week, he told us. Hell, by then, my pa said, he'll be all petered out." The boy grinned big. "You get it? Old man, young woman?"

"I got it. You a good pilot?"

"I make it back and forth," the boy said, kind of cocky.

"Fine. All I want is across. I'm looking for a guy, about thirty, black beard, calls himself Terry."

"Lots of folks use the ferry and I don't know all their names. I sure don't remember him."

"He'd've gone over in the last few days."

The boy shook his head and went to stoking the boiler with large chunks of wood. Slocum settled back for the ride, seated on the bench beside the firebox. The captain soon climbed up to the steering wheel deck and set the ferry in reverse. Once in the dark river, he turned the boat around and headed for the distant lanterns hung at the other dock. The current slapped the hollow sides of the vessel. Spray

151

flew over them from the paddle wheel churning up the Snake.

Wrapped in a blanket, Slocum moved around Whistler's Post, like one of the resident Indians. He slumped down and sat on the porch. He could hear Merle Hubbard's loud voice and the tinny piano. When he looked in the grimy glass window and studied the occupants from the sides so he wasn't apparent, no one who even resembled Terry was in the room. Hubbard had some girl with him at the bar and was running the big ham of his hand over her butt.

Slocum went back and found the bay. He rode north under the stars.

Sun was making a pink streak in the east. Matty's brown collies barked when he rode up to the cow lot and listened to the two streams of milk on the tin bucket. Dismounting, he came over to the pole gate and leaned on it, looking at her ramrod back as she held her head high, seated beside the belly of the brindle cow.

"So, bossy," she said softly. "See you made it back. Find her?"

"Yes, I did."

"Didn't bring her back?"

"No, she's got a new man."

She scooted the bucket back and looked at the contents. "He must be a stud horse."

"How's that?" he asked.

"After being with you, bet she found that most men are made lots smaller." She rose and he slipped into the pen to take the pail of milk from her.

"Never went to bed with her."

She blinked and shook her head in disbelief. Then she ran her finger by her nose, after which she dug a rag out of her dress pocket to blow it. "Something's making my nose run. Where you going now?" she asked.

"Looking for a whiskey trader named Terry. Sold some Cayuse liquor and they went on the warpath down there." He looked at the small house ahead.

"Put the pail on the table, and I'll fix you some breakfast and you can sleep in the shed. Don't reckon you had any in awhile—sleep, that is?"

"No, sleep sounds good. What about the children?"

"They won't tell him nothing."

"I didn't come here to cause you any trouble."

She looked up at him and gave him a crooked smile. Under her breath she imitated her husband in a coarse voice, "Who's that sumbitch beat the hell out of me? He said you know his name. How did you know his name, woman, is what I'd like to know."

"What did you tell him?" He used both hands to put the three-quarters-full pail on the table.

"Stay home and do some work around here, you can learn a lot."

"If I—"

She wrinkled her nose than blew it again in the rag. "I can survive without him. My eggs, butter and hogs make more money than he does anyway. He blows his wheat money and runs a bar bill up against the next one."

She carried the pot over and poured him coffee. "I still haven't got to town to buy me some material. Kathren's man came by and took in my eggs and butter and drew my supplies."

"She all right?"

Matty cut a look at him. "I think she's going to marry Howard next month."

"Good. She told me he was sour on women after his wife left him."

"Now, ain't that something. I heard that story, too. His wife went off to work in a cathouse." She cracked some eggs in a bowl, then rustled up the fire in her stove under the cast-iron skillet. "Might not be any worse than being stuck out here on a poor farm." She looked out the open front door and stared for a long while. "Might not have been such a bad idea." Then she laughed and deftly sliced off some snow-white fatback. "Course he couldn't keep one wife, he might not keep another."

"You acted like you expected me back." He watched her through the coffee vapors.

She twisted and nodded, satisfied. "I kinda dreamed one night you'd ride by going or coming from somewhere."

"What else you dream about?"

"Going to rain tomorrow." The meat sizzling in the skillet, she turned around with her hands on her narrow hips, then wiped them on the apron. "And that man you want—Terry— rode by here yesterday. Kind of a hard case."

"Thanks."

She raised her chin up. "He buys whiskey from a man named Yurbacon."

"How far away is he?"

"Oh, about ten miles. North and east of Kathren's place. I thought you might have run into him coming down here."

Slocum shook his head.

Looking at the loft, then acting satisfied, she picked up a plate and leaned over close to him. Her whisper in his ear was direct. "You leave right off looking for him, I'll sure be mad."

Slocum stretched his arms over his head to flex his stiff back. "I guess he can wait."

A small smile of relief tugged at the corners of her tight mouth, and she went back to tend to her cooking.

"Howard told me there's been lots of word on Injun trouble down in Oregon," she said, putting the plate heaping with fried potatoes, scrambled eggs and side meat before him. "Knowed you was coming, I'd've made biscuits."

"Looks wonderful."

"Starving man ain't hard to pacify."

He started to take the first bite off his fork.

Strait backed in the cane-bottom chair opposite him, she asked, "Where you headed after you find Terry?"

"He's the whiskey trader stirred up the Cayuses and got those people killed. He needs to answer for his crime."

"Looks like a tough customer."

"Ain't they all?"

She reached over, grasped his forearm and squeezed it for a second. Then she looked at the loft and dropped her gaze to her lap. Her words were very low. "I act like a silly schoolgirl, don't I?"

"No, you never had a chance to be one." He cut the browned potatoes with the side of his fork.

"That's right."

"Mom?"

She sprung from the chair and answered the sleepy-eyed boy who looked over the edge of the loft.

"Time to get up?"

"Yes."

"Come on, Violia," he said to his sister. Soon the pair descended the ladder and nodded politely when she introduced "Mr. Slocum."

He washed down breakfast with another cup of coffee. By then his eyelids were weighted with lead, his belly full from her tasty food.

"I'll head for the shed," he said. "We can talk more later."

She agreed, busy dishing out oatmeal to her children.

In the morning coolness he crossed the yard, listening to a rooster brag and the milk cow low to a couple of calves. His bay was munching on hay in the lot, and he felt a few hours' sleep would revive him. The shed's interior smelled musty, so he propped open the door, since the dirty four-pane window was stationary.

The mattress spread out, he shed his boots and hung the gunbelt on a nail beside where his head would lay. When he sat on the narrow bed, the ropes creaked and the notion of sleep's arms came over him like a great wish being granted. In minutes, he was in that other world.

Smell of chloroform filled his nose. He could hear people talking nearby.

"What chance he got, Doc?"

"Not much in my opinion."

"He's got to live."

"Got a good reason?"

"Yeah, he's worth five hundred bucks alive in Fort Scott, Kansas."

"Hmm. Most posters on wanted men say dead or alive."

"Not this one."

"Well, Mr. Abbott, I'll see what I can do. Now clear the hell out and let me and my assistant do our job."

"I'll stay—"

"Get the hell out of here! I'm damn tired of looking at

you. That man ain't going anywhere shot up like he is . . ."

"Yes, I am! Yes, I am!" Slocum screamed, but neither man heard him. They went about preparing themselves for his surgery. He saw the enamel pan in the assistant's hand, the shiny knives and probes laid out on a white towel.

"Hope he makes it," Doc said and rolled up his sleeves.

"I'm alive! I'm alive—"

"Wake up. You've been screaming," Matty said in his face.

He raised up on his elbows. "Guess I was having a bad dream."

"Whatever it was, you sure wanted them to believe you were alive."

She put her skirt under her and sat on the edge of the cot. With a clean rag, she wiped his forehead and face dry, a look of concern written on her smooth face.

"You better try to sleep some more."

He sat up and rubbed the grit from the corners of his eyes. "Aw, I've had enough for now."

"Couldn't be over four or five." Her blue eyes focused on the open doorway.

"If I didn't have kids, would you take me with you?"

"No," he said softly. "Where one survives, two might not. Besides a woman needs a roof over her head. Sky is not the answer for shingles in her mind."

"You can't keep on riding forever."

He closed his eyes and braced his arms behind himself. "You're right, but I can't endanger you, the boy and girl, either, by staying here very long."

She twisted and looked hard at him. "I know that—" Then she gave a hard exhale. "But don't hurry off this time."

"We'll see. I may ride up and scout this Yurbacon's deal."

"He's got a covered wagon and I think a shack. He sold Merle enough whiskey to build a mansion."

"I want to have a look-see. You have a telescope?"

"Yes. I'll get it."

"Thanks."

She paused in the doorway. "I killed two chickens. You'll be back for supper, won't you?"

"Sure. And thanks, Matty."

She dismissed his gratitude with a head shake and in a swirl of her skirt was gone. He noticed her hemline was high enough for him to see her brogan shoes, so she didn't have to carry the dress. A practical working woman needed that freedom. He closed his dry eyes and hoped for a flood to water them. None came, so he pulled on his boots and prepared to go locate the bootlegger.

He saddled the chestnut and led him out of the pen. He noticed the bald-faced colt was gone. Perhaps her oldest had taken him over to the ranch where he worked. She came from the house with a plate.

"Made some bread this morning while you were asleep." She held out the offering of buttered dark bread slices with red jam.

"Currants," she announced.

"Good," he said, between bites.

She stood, holding the plate for him while he ate the offering. She was kind of stiff-looking in the afternoon sun, but the rich rye bread filled up lots of room and the tangy jelly made the treat even better.

When he finished, she took the small telescope out of her dress pocket. "Here. Stay far away from them."

"I'd almost kiss you for both the bread and this."

Her backbone looked as if it straightened even more. "Impossible. But keep that thought."

"I will, Matty, I surely will."

"Use that scope."

He put the brass case in his saddlebags and then mounted the bay. "I will." A salute and he rode off.

He skirted Kathren's place. With her preparing to marry Howard, no need in him disturbing them. So far he'd seen no sign of anyone riding east toward where he expected to find the moonshiner, in the tracks that paralleled the Columbia on the first bench. Then he came upon the hoof prints where someone had gone that way, and there were even traces of a wagon using the dim tracks in times past. He swung the stout gelding in that direction and looked for smoke or any sign.

Clouds had begun to gather. Perhaps her dream it would rain was right. He eased his way, stopping under ridges and peering carefully over the tops so he didn't ride in on them. Soon he noted a line of cottonwoods. Must be a creek there, he decided. Whiskey makers needed water to cool their coils and distill off the alcohol. Good enough.

He left the horse hobbled in a grassy draw and took the rifle and scope to set out afoot. His first view of the creek offered nothing. Then the scope caught sight of a horse grazing and he smiled. The pony had saddle marks on his withers and showed a square patch on his back where sweat had dried from a blanket. He moved on, and in the next peek over the hilltop, he found the sun-browned canvas top of the wagon.

An Indian woman chopped firewood. Her colorful dress of red, blue and orange showed without the glass. An unfamiliar man walked through camp smoking a pipe, and some small breed children ran about playing. No sign of Terry. But he could be down there. Slocum suspected the horse that had been ridden so hard had been the man's mount. Of course, he could be sitting on the ground, too, in camp and Slocum not able at the distance to see him.

A well-staked-down canvas fly served as their shelter. No shack in sight either. He could see boards laid across barrels for tables. No doubt that was where they bottled the lightning. Then he caught a hint of wood smoke and knew they must be running off a batch. It also explained why the woman was so busy chopping up wood.

Her arms loaded, she carried a large amount over to where the wagon blocked his vision. If only he could catch sight of—Then he saw two figures come and stand under the fly. One was the pipe smoker, and the black-bearded one looked enough like Terry to satisfy Slocum.

Next question. If Terry knew nothing about the posse's operation, he might be there to buy more whiskey. Very well, Terry could know nothing. Word of the roundup wasn't at the ferry when he arrived there or that cocky boy pilot would have talked about it. It might all work to his advantage—if Terry would ride south when he got his goods.

Must not be much law in this part of Washington—nothing at Whistler's resembled it. Two men, he could handle. If he only knew how long they had to finish working the batch, it would be better. Still, they had to ride past her place. He'd make some more plans when the time came. Meanwhile, a little rest and relaxation wouldn't hurt him.

A few good nights' sleep sounded wonderful, because once the Terry deal was settled, he'd for sure have to ride on. Not looking forward to that, he hiked back, found his horse and rode him for Matty's.

"You find the man you were looking for?" she asked, seated across from him and dishing out brown crusted chicken on the plate of mash potatoes and green beans.

He accepted the dish from her and nodded. "Yeah, they're up there."

The children were already in the loft, supposedly asleep. Her candles flickered and smoked.

"Used sheep grease to make them candles." She indicated the light and shook her head in disgust. "Never again. Besides it smells bad. Sorry."

"Nothing's going to ruin this evening. I thought all afternoon about it and on the ride back, how good this would taste."

She shook her head to dismiss his words and looked in her lap. "All I thought was, *He ain't coming back.*"

"I told you—"

"I know, but ain't much in my life ever worked out the way I wanted it."

"So, this is mighty good chicken." He waved his half-consumed breast at her.

"Have I messed up your plans? I mean asking you to come back."

He paused with the coffee cup inches from his lips. "No. I'm looking forward to it. I'll reshoe the bay. Do some repairs on the saddle. A little time like this means a lot."

The corners of her mouth turned up pleased, and she nodded stiffly. "Good. You won't be disappointed."

The meal over, her dishes done, she came out under a

shawl to where he sat on a bench in the night wind. A coyote yipped and she made a frown. "I've shot four of them chicken getters so far this summer."

"Probably raised six more," he said resting his elbows on his knees.

She laughed, free-sounding. "Yeah, and out there making more right now."

"I need a bath."

"Why didn't you say so? I'd've heated water."

"I figured the kids and all, it might be inconvenient." He stood up and stretched. "Get a pail and some soap. I can do it by the trough."

"Oh, that's cold. That water from the hand pump is really cold even after setting all day in the sun."

"Get the pail. I can take it."

She hurried inside and was back by the time he stood up.

"We'll see how tough you are." They hurried for the trough that stuck inside the pen. Short of breath, they both bent over to catch theirs with hands on their knees. He looked over at her.

"You'll get your dress all wet, pouring water on me."

"No, I won't," she said and began undoing the buttons down the front.

He toed off his boots, hung his holster on the fence. He raced with her to undress. She stripped away her dress, then her camisole, and hung them on the fence. He finished and hung his clothes on the rail on the other side of the trough. The pearly starlight shone on her slender fanny.

She turned and shook her head in disapproval. "I don't know, Slocum. I do the most damn awful foolish things with you."

"But ain't it fun?" He took the pail, dipped it full, then held it over his head and dumped it on himself. The cold shock stopped his heart for a split second and he sucked in his breath.

"Soap?" He held out his hand, but she was laughing too hard to give it to him.

"My gosh, Slocum, I wished you could have heard your-self sucking in your breath—"

Then she moved in and began to soap his body. The lather soon made him look like a snowman, and she left no parts unwashed, though some she lingered over and he kissed her for. At last, looking him in the eye, she asked, "You ready to scream?"

"Yes."

She climbed on the edge of the wood tank and dipped out the first one. "Here goes."

The cold splash numbed him in an instant, then the wind swept his wet skin and he shivered working away the soap as she repeated the process. Soon the water felt warmer than the air.

She jumped down and began to rub him dry with a sack towel. Goose bumps popped out on his back and arms, but her brisk efforts helped. He hugged her and they kissed. Then he swept her up in his arms and carried her toward the shed.

She on the bed, he settled beside her, he pushed the hair back from her face as if discovering her for the first time. His hand cupped the small mound on her rib cage and the nipple responded to the touch of his palm.

Their mouths soon became ignited, and he moved on top of her, then between her long slender legs that she raised for him. His turgid shaft eased inside her doorway, and she drew her shoulders together and sighed in pleasure.

With her strong arms she forced him down on top of her and hugged him as if she couldn't get enough.

"My God, Slocum don't quit!" she cried in his ear. "I want you to do this forever and ever." She arched her back toward him and they went off into the waves of pleasure. His skin-tight erection pounding her, the walls of her vagina swelled and grew closer.

Air became a scarce commodity in their lungs. Dazzled as if caught in a tornado's force, they pressed on, until at last she cried out loud and he felt his guns deep inside go off, too.

They lay in a heap. Spent, drained and weary, they slept in each other's arms.

He awoke and listened, with it still dark outside. Easing himself off the cot and away from the warmth of her, he went barefooted across the gritty floor to the doorway. In the night, a tired horse coughed—not his.

Who the hell was out there? A second horse, too.

His saddle was on the fence, ten long steps from the shack's doorway. In the moonlight he could see it. If he could locate the intruders, there might be one chance in ten that he could get over there and jerk the Winchester out of the scabbard and . . .

20

In the dim light he saw that both of the riders were hatless and carrying rifles. They rode slow-like toward the house, and once they were a few yards past him, he broke for the corral. His bare soles stepped on sharp things, but he managed to jerk out the rifle and fire two quick shots. A red blaze marked the barrel's end each time, and the gunsmoke billowed up in his face.

A horse screamed and went down. Then the buck ran and jumped on the back of the other horse and the two rode pell-mell out of the yard. Slocum knelt down and took two more shots, but he knew they were futile.

She rushed out the shed wrapped in a blanket. "You all right?"

"Yes."

"Got to see about my kids. They'll be scared to death." She raced off to the house.

"They'll be fine. They touched nothing," he said after her.

She never wavered and ran inside. He could hear her talking to the children as he dressed by the tank. He better hook up her team of draft horses and drag off that dead horse before the kids saw it.

Who were they anyway? Some more worthless renegades up to no good, and where was her dog? Had they already killed it? Hard to say. He headed for the house, checking the rounds in his six-gun as he went. Why did he have the idea in the back of his mind that those two were the Cayuse killers of Little Wayne?

Why would they be going back up that way? He stopped. Squaw and Able. Damn, those two could have cut across country another way and been headed to Crab Creek. He'd not gone back to Cross Creek to find out what they did.

If Squaw and Able were back on Crab Creek, then those Cayuse killers were headed for them. He better trail them. She appeared in the doorway, wearing a faded dress and carrying her milk pail by the bail in the crook of her arm. Passing the dead paint horse lying on the ground, she shook her head in disgust and hurried by it.

"How are the children?"

"Fine. They'll be all right. Thanks to you. I never felt threatened up here before." Her thin shoulders quaked under the material. "I will from now on."

"I think they're the ones kidnapped the Cayuse woman."

"What're they doing up here?" She swept the hair back from her face in the wind's gathering forces.

"Looking for her again, I guess." He searched around. "I think they may have killed your dog."

"Why—"

"To silence him."

She closed her eyes. "I was so happy last night—now this. I guess I should have been more alert. I usually hear things."

"Don't blame yourself. I'm going to track them—have to."

"I understand. Can you wait till I milk the cow? I'll make some breakfast—" She shook her head in defeat, realizing he must move on. "Help yourself to the bread and butter on the table. And Slocum—come by again before you leave this land."

Seeing the plea written on her face, he reached over and kissed her cheek. "I'll try, Matty. No promises."

"Be careful anyway," she said after him.

Slocum reached Kathren's place mid-morning. She was hanging clothes on a line in the strong wind.

"Slocum." She used her hand to sweep the hair back from her face. "How nice to see you."

"Seen any signs of some renegades?"

"Yes, they stole two horses, and Howard has gone after them. I'm quite concerned about him. He's not a big gun man."

"How long ago?"

"Maybe an hour. Are you going after them, too?"

"Yes."

"Good," she said with a look of relief. "I'm certain he can use all the help you can give him."

With a salute for her, he set the horse into a long lope. He'd been holding back for fear that he might ride over them. No time for holding back now. He pushed the horse harder. They flew across the sagebrush sea on the rise above the wide Columbia, reflecting silver mirrorlike images as it rolled past.

He let him walk to cool, and stood in the stirrups. Howard and the renegades couldn't be much farther. Tracks and sign were fresh. They couldn't be over thirty minutes ahead of him.

When he topped the next rise, he saw gunsmoke, then he heard the pops. Howard needed him. He set the gelding into a hard run, urging him on. No more shots. He wondered should he draw the rifle or use his Colt. The rifle was the most accurate at any distance. He topped the next hill and saw the two bucks standing over a downed man.

He drew up and took aim with the Winchester. His first shot sprayed sand all over the two Indians. They fled for their horses. He charged in after them, and watched them mount up and tear away.

Of course, they rode fresher horses, and the bay was beginning to falter when he reined him up. He dismounted beside the fallen Howard, with a wary eye after the departing bucks making lots of dust in the wind.

The man, in his thirties, looked pained when he sat up holding his left arm. Blood had begun to seep through his fingers when Slocum knelt beside him. Clean-shaven, his face paled underneath the suntan, his blue eyes furious. Howard looked stout enough to Slocum to endure his wound.

"Where did you come from?" He looked up at Slocum.

"Kathren said you'd gone after them."

"Damn, I couldn't even catch two dumb Indian horse thieves right." He shook his head ruefully.

"Ain't no right way to do that." Slocum looked after their dust. "Those two outdid me a couple of times, too." He squatted beside the man and took his arm, gently lifting it. "Let me cut that sleeve. I need to see how bad you're shot up."

"Makes me mad. I should have killed them."

Slocum used the great knife from the sheath behind his back and sliced the shirtsleeve open. When he lifted it, Howard winced his left cheek under his eye in obvious pain.

"Ain't easy to kill someone the first time." Slocum could see the wound's exit hole. Satisfied, he let the arm down and cut the material to make a tourniquet.

"Yeah," Howard grunted and squeezed his left forearm with his right hand. "I hate killing anything."

"Except out here, sometimes it's do or die." He fastened the strip above the wound and made it tight as he could. "The bullet went plumb through your arm. This twist should stop the bleeding till we can get you back home."

"What about those two?" Howard looked impatient with the idea of their escape.

"I know where they're going. I'll get them. You're more important right now than they are."

"I'd damn sure like my horse stock back."

"I'll try to do that, too."

"What's your line of work, Slocum?" he asked as Slocum helped him to his feet.

"Cowboy, when I can find work."

He gathered Howard's big horse and his own. To make it easier on the man, he put him on the chestnut and he rode the tall one.

"You know Kathren," Howard said as they walked their horses.

"We've met."

"You know she's agreed to marry me?"

"Good woman. You're lucky."

"My last one ran off," Howard said as if talking to the wind. "Guess I've been thinking about that ever since." He shook his head, made a face and reached for his arm in pain. "Why—would a woman do that?"

Slocum shook his head. "You know I figured out a long time ago, you can't change other people. They're going to do what possesses them. Crazy as it seems, dumb or whatever. Only one person you can change is yourself."

"I kinda came to that conclusion. Been dumb of me not noticing Kathren—anyone else would have already left me."

Slocum glanced over at him as they rode the tracks between the sagebrush. "You're going to make it."

"You talking about this damn arm, or me and her?"

Slocum twisted in the saddle and looked over his shoulder for the renegades' dust. Nothing. They were long gone. He turned back to the man. "I mean both."

"Good. Bad as it hurts I may not want to make it." Then he laughed and Slocum did, too.

21

"He's sleeping," Kathren said and came out on the dark porch where Slocum sat. "The bleeding's stopped. The burnt flour helped, I think, stop the bleeding. Maybe he can sleep awhile."

She used both hands to hold the loose hair back from her face, standing at the edge of the log stoop, facing into the night wind. Her tall, willowy figure in the blue print dress was framed like an orange cutout in the lamplight shining out the door casing.

"He was disappointed he couldn't apprehend those two."

She looked back at him and nodded. "He said that three times tonight: He should have shot both of them."

"He'll make a good man, Kathren. While I didn't know him before, I'd say that he's someone finding himself."

"Yes," she said softly and dropped her gaze.

"I'll go on in the morning and find them. Try to get his ponies back. He ever find anybody to help him clear ground?"

"Yes, two families are coming. Norwegians. They didn't have much on their homesteads from the way he talked, and were afraid with winter coming on they'd starve out. Should be here in a few days."

"Good," Slocum said with his elbows on his knees.

"Where will you go?"

"Wherever the wind takes me."

"Sounds exciting."

"I'd trade places with Howard any minute."

She turned and stepped over to put her back to the wall. "Be nice to see something beside purple sage, smell it every day and listen to coyotes wail at night."

"Sleep in wet blankets, eat moldy dry cheese, have your horse give out and walk the soles off your boots in a land full of stickers and burrs."

"Guess I'll take the sagebrush then and hope that those sticks I'm watering will make big trees before I'm too old to see them."

"They will, Kathren. They will." He gazed at the million stars overhead. Come morning, he needed to get after those two and recover Howard's horses. Then Terry—had the whiskey man started back for Oregon? No telling. Those two Cayuse were the biggest threat to Squaw and Able. Terry was really more of a nuisance with the renegades all rounded up.

He couldn't forget Carter and Ward. They must be sniffing out his backtrail by this time, since he didn't show up at Cross Creek with the posse's return. Life for him never got much better—though every once in a while he found a few days' solace.

He closed his eyes and flexed his stiff shoulders. Morning would come early, better find his bedroll. When he stood up, she stepped over in front of him. She put her arms around him and kissed him softly on the mouth.

"Thanks for saving him for me. They'd've killed him if you hadn't rode up when you did. We owe you."

Slocum tasted the honey on his lips and shook his head. "I've been well paid. Clothes, saddle you gave me. And the rest."

She hugged him tight and pressed her cheek to his. "Thanks for all you've done. If you hadn't came along when you did, I think I might have left him while he was gone."

They parted like a great gate opening the space between them. He thought for a minute about her long, turgid breasts and the smooth sweep of her waistline. Then he drew in a deep noseful of sage. Good woman. Kathren would make a wonderful grandmother sitting in a rocker peeling apples and telling her grandkids about those early days, when renegades stole Grandpa Howard's new horses.

Next morning, she brought him coffee and a plate of food about the time he finished saddling his horse. He hitched the reins on the corral and nodded to her.

"You'll never know," she said, folding her arms.

He sat the coffee on a block of wood and squatted down to eat. "What's that?"

She gave kick at the dust with her shoe. "How many times last night I almost came out here to find you."

"I'm flattered," he said around his full mouth, and waved the fork at her. "You've got obligations now."

She hugged her arms and walked back and forth. "You know he's still never made love to me?"

"Go easy. It may be fragile, at first, but you can win. You're gonna win."

She raised her face to the first light and threw her head back. "You're sure?"

"Certain. I wouldn't want to sound nasty, but you could wake up an eighty-year-old man and make him take notice."

She laughed. "I hope he's not that old—I mean—"

"Hey, I savvy. Good food." He waved a forkful at her.

She nodded that she heard him. "Anyway, he slept well last night."

"Make him rest. Put that arm in a sling, and the first sign of any infection, you burn that wound out."

She made a face. "With gunpowder?"

"Tough treatment, but it's all I know. Isn't any doctor at Whistler's is there?"

"No."

"If I get the horses, I should be back in less than week. Any men come asking about me, hang a pair of red underwear on your line, so I don't ride in on them."

"Be glad to."

He handed her the plate, then took the coffee cup and rose. "Kathren, I'm wishing you the best."

"I may need it." She forced a smile, but her long lashes

were wet when he swung up in the saddle and waved good-bye to her.

At sundown, he crossed over the Mustang Mountains and looked back at the blood red snake that the Columbia made far below. In the west was the snow pile of Mount Rainier. He pushed the bay downhill.

Weary and the horse tiring, he stopped and hobbled him in a coulee, out of the wind. He chewed on some jerky and dry cheese and at last lay down in his bedroll. He wondered how Able and Squaw were making it as he drifted off into sleep.

Before dawn, he watered the bay at a seep and headed downhill. When he came into view of the green willows, he checked his Colt. Rolling the cylinder on his shirtsleeve, he let the hammer rest on the empty one and reholstered it.

The tent looked like it had been tightened and restaked, but no sign of anyone or horses. He looked at the prints about the camp and discovered that Howard's horses had been there before him. With a head shake, he dropped out of the saddle, loosened the cinch and led the horse to water. After he finished drinking, Slocum made the decision that their tracks went east, probably to round up the geldings. The two Cayuse were on the same trail.

He jerked the latigos up tight and swung in the seat. The bay horse better have some bottom left in him. Able and Squaw might be in real trouble if they didn't have their guard up. If they were daydreaming along, those two killers might surprise and hurt them.

He sent the boy through the creek on the run. He needed to be at that horse trap quick as he could get there. The horse, revived by the water, flew through the sage, flushing prairie chickens and grouse that boomed off in salute to them. The dip in the long line of hills over the pens looked in the hazy distance to be a long ways away. But they were headed there—so he wasn't too late, Slocum hoped.

After an hour's hard run, he pulled the hard-breathing gelding down to a hard walk. His guts roiled. He hoped that nothing happened to the two of them—his greatest concern.

A jackrabbit popped up—the big horse snorted and side-stepped.

Slocum patted his sweaty neck. "You are still alive, old pony."

The mid-morning sun was climbing high when at last he saw the cleft in the hills. At the mouth of the canyon, he slipped off the horse, jerked the Winchester out of the scabbard and started forward on foot, his eyes scanning the tops of the steep sides for any sign of the Indians.

Then a shot rang out, the muffled sound of a pistol. He began to run. Another answered and someone shouted. Sounded like they were hit. He dropped the lever down, and seeing that the bright metallic cartridge was in place, he snapped the chamber shut, never missing a step.

His breath growing shorter, he rounded the pen and saw the two Indians at the corral gates aiming and shooting at something inside. He made a sharp stop, took a deep breath and drew the rifle's stock to his shoulder.

"Throw down your guns!"

The squat-built Tall Horse whirled around with a pistol in his fist, the black rage painted on his face. Slocum's finger instinctively squeezed the trigger. Smoke curled out of the muzzle of the Winchester after the fingernail-size piece of hot lead left the barrel. Struck hard in the chest, the Indian was thrown backward by the force of the bullet, like a freight train had hit him. Hard enough that Slocum saw the bottoms of his moccasins turned out toward him when Horse's back was slammed into the corral panels. Like a limp rag, he hit on his butt next, with his head crumpled over like his neck was broke.

"Stop!" Slocum shouted to the fleeing Dog. The Indian never looked back, headed down the canyon. And never slowed when Slocum's bullet struck the dirt beside his feet and made a cloud of dust.

"You aren't stealing my horse!" Slocum shouted as the gap between the two grew greater.

Walnut stock to his cheek, he drew a bead where suspenders would cross on the back of a man. His long hair streaming behind him, Dog put on more speed. But he would never outrun the bullet. Hit, he straightened his spine and then pitched forward to roll several times ass over teakettle.

Slocum shook his head. Those two needed to die. They made their own decision. He glanced down at the still body of Tall Horse. Little Wayne was revenged.

"Hey, you all right?" he shouted, looking around for the pair.

"Yeah, what took you so long to get here?" Able said, unfolding from behind the rocks. Soon she popped up, too, brushing herself off and grinning like a possum.

Slocum shook his head at the pair, relieved to see they were all right. "I thought maybe one of you was shot."

"Piece of lead skinned me was all," Able said. "It sure burned."

Slocum looked at the herd of familiar geldings in the far end of the trap, snorting and shuffling. "I see you two can capture horses."

"Hey, she told me you cut them. They all survived, but one bald-faced one is missing. She said he was a good one."

"I traded him and some money to Matty Hubbard for her son's horse. He was a little young."

"I see. Well, Nomie and I are going to break out this bunch and gather some more so by next spring we got us a herd and can go down there on the reservation and claim us a good ranch in the Blue Mountains."

"You have to be married—"

"Yeah, well, Mom kinda put her foot down about that. We got married at Cross Creek before we came up here." Able smiled big.

"Very well. We better dig a grave for them." He used his thumb over his shoulder to indicate the Cayuse.

Able looked off that way and nodded. "I'll have to bring a shovel back."

Slocum frowned as Squaw ran down to the body of Running Dog, turned him over and soon let out a cry. "Got the money back!"

Able frowned at Slocum and shook his head.

"Some outlaw robbed another one and he died and she found it," Slocum said. Good enough explanation. If she wanted him to know more, she'd tell him herself about Wayne.

"You must mean 'Wine.' She called him that."

"Wayne, but you ain't missed much."

"Guess not," Able said as she hurried back with the sack.

"Give half to Slocum," she said, handing the money sack to Able.

Slocum held out his hands. "No. You two will need it to build your ranch."

"Nope. If you hadn't had the trust in me to go with you, I'd never have met her. And you saved our skin here and all you did for her. We want you to have half of it." They both nodded and looked at him expectantly.

He shrugged and then relented. Might as well not argue.

Able sat on the ground and began to count out the shiney coins in stacks of fifty. Sun glinted off the yellow rounds with their sharply grooved edges.

She hung onto Slocum's arm and nodded her approval. "You take half."

"I don't need it."

"Yes, you need it."

"Comes to six-fifty." Able scrambled to his feet and began collecting piles. "Here, there's three-twenty-five." Slocum filled his vest pockets with the coins, still insisting they keep the loot. No use. He'd find a place the money was needed down the road.

"I'll get our horses," Able said. "We can leave these in the trap overnight. And don't worry, I'll bury them two in the morning."

"We need to get those two horses they rode in on. They stole them from Kathren and Howard. I promised to get them back."

"Bet they're up on the ridge. We can swing by that way going out."

Slocum nodded, and with her hanging on his arm, they went for his bay.

"How is the wife business going?" he asked her.

She raised her chin up and smiled big, showing her even teeth. "That boy, him want plenty *nicky-do*."

"Figures."

"Whew," she sighed and shook her head. "Him plenty good man for Cayuse squaw."

"You two can catch your horse herd this winter and then you can go home."

"Yeah, yeah. You need to come then. I make new white dress from elk skin and put many beads on it to wear when I ride in there." She thrust her small breasts against the beadwork on her top.

"I bet that you'll be the prettiest wife on the reservation."

She put a concerned look on her face. "If me not too big then for new dress." With a head shake for her concerns over the matter, she used her hands to make a big circle in front of her belly.

They both laughed.

22

If he could round up Terry and get him into McGrim's jurisdiction, then he could leave the Northwest. His mind was more on shapely, brown-skinned señoritas dancing to hard-plucked guitar music, the sounds of trumpets playing Latin songs. He dreamed of drinking *cerveza* and tequila in the lacy shade of a mesquite tree in San Antonio. The last few cool nights told him enough that winter would soon sweep into this country. Patches of snow would remain in the shade of the sagebrush. Ice would edge the creek's shores and frost coat the tents' canvas. He had the leads of the two horses he planned to return to Kathren and Howard. At least he could take their stock back to them.

All he needed to do was look to the west and see Mount Rainier in its year-round dress of white to know there wasn't as much as a barb-wire fence between this country and the North Pole. He drew in a deep breath and pulled the latigo tight.

"You can stay here and take half the horses," Able offered, with her clutching his arm.

"No, I need to find Terry and get moving."

"Them bounty hunters still after you?"

"They could be." Slocum shrugged away the notion of their pursuit and threaded the leather through the D ring.

"You sure don't sound worried about them."

"If it wasn't them, Able, be some other dang fool."

"Been a pleasure to know you. You sure helped me and her." The boy shook his head. "We could never repay you."

He clapped with both hands on the heavy-weighted coins in his vest. "You gave me too much as it is."

She rushed in and squeezed him in a bear hug.

"Take care of each other, that's what I want," he said, looking down and tousling her braids.

"We will," they promised, holding each other like each was afraid the other might get away.

He stepped aboard and nodded. "You take care." And rode off.

When he climbed the far bank and looked back—arm in arm, they were headed in a big hurry to get back inside the tent. He nodded his approval and smiled. He better get back and find Terry, then head south. Those Mexican tunes were in his brain. The morning sun overhead wasn't as strong as before either. He jerked on the two lead horses to catch up.

He crossed the crest before the sun set, and camped along the rolling Columbia, taking a bath in the still cold shallows and letting his clothes dry spread over some bushes. His driftwood fire made a radiant heat to dry in front of as he sat naked on the ground. He listened to the coyotes wail at the night sky and ate the last of his jerky and cheese before his clothes were dry enough to put on again.

He slept a few hours and then, before the sun came up, headed for Yurbacon's camp. He needed to put a stop to those whiskey men if all they could do was sell their rotgut to renegade Indians.

In the half-light of predawn, he hobbled the two spare horses at a distance and prepared for his ride into their camp. The chestnut came off the steep slope toward the wagon under the cottonwoods, rocking Slocum from side to side in the saddle. He rounded the canvas-topped rig with the rifle in his hands, looking for the men.

An Indian woman jumped up from her cooking fire, screaming as if in fear.

"Shut up!" Slocum said to her, and still saw no sight of Terry and Yurbacon.

"Where is he?" he demanded, meaning Yurbacon.

The heavyset woman stood back from her cooking fire. Her jowls shook when she jerked her head up to glare at him with her cold, black eyes. Hands on her ample hips, she raised up to challenge him.

"Not here," she said with a sneer.

"Where did he go?" Slocum saw the dark eyes of the four small children, under blankets, peering at him from beneath the wagon's box.

She shook her head to dismiss him. "No say."

"Which child you want me to shoot first?" Slocum asked, shifting his weight in the saddle to glance down at them.

"No shoot my children. He went with the white man to Oregon."

"How long ago?" He cocked the hammer back on the Winchester. It made an audible click to enforce his threat.

"One day ago. They took two pack mules," she said quickly, but her concerned look kept darting to the little ones.

"I won't kill any this time. But you better pack and go home."

"Why?" She raised up, straightened her thick shoulders and pushed her large breasts forward under the purple blouse.

" 'Cause he's going to prison and soon the snow will blow. You have horses for the wagon?"

"Yes."

"Use them to get out of here. He won't be coming back for you." Slocum shook his head at her in warning. "He will be in prison."

"Prison?" she said, as if trying the word on her tongue for the first time. Then she nodded that she understood him and dropped her gaze to the ground.

He started to leave. Thinking it over, he reached along the horse and dug out a gold coin. "Buy them young'uns some candy with this."

He pitched the coin toward her and the round twenty-dollar piece landed near her feet. She blinked her dark lashes at him in disbelief, then bent over to retrieve it.

He swung the bay horse around and headed back toward the river for the other two. The whiskey makers were a day's ride ahead of him. Good enough. They'd be headed for

Oregon. Terry still might not know the Cayuse renegades were all rounded up, and that might fit Slocum's plans fine.

In the distance, he spotted red underwear flapping on Kathren's clothesline when he crested the hill. Immediately, he wheeled his horse and the others around and rode up the coulee under the rise to circle for a better look before he rode in. Damn—the bounty hunters must have found his trail.

Could be a coincidence, the underwear on the line, but he doubted it. Worse yet, he hated to waste half a day waiting for darkness, but for insurance sake, he decided not to go in until sundown. The horses hobbled, out of sight, so they could graze, he began to make his way stealthfully toward the homestead. He could see no sign of any horses near the shack, but some of the sheds were in the way of his vision.

Belly down, he crawled closer, listening. No sign of anyone, then he spotted Howard with his arm in a sling. The man disappeared into the barn. Slocum moved that way until he was behind the open-ended structure. Easing his way along, he climbed a rail pen and pressed his back to the rough boards.

With his ear to the wall, he could hear someone hand scooping grain. Slow-like, he moved to toward the door and then a figure appeared. Slocum's fist tightened on the grips of the Colt.

"Oh!" Howard said. "It's you. We've been worried about you. Two men came by asking about you."

Slocum shook his head. "They still here?"

"No, they rode back to Whistler's last night. But she hung the red underwear out hoping you would see it and not ride in on them."

Slocum holstered the Colt. "Thanks. Carter and Ward?"

"Two cowboys. Looked like drovers."

"That's them. What did they say?"

"Said they knew you were up here. The boy runs the ferry said you'd crossed the river. They talked about you probably being with some Indian whore."

"They need their mouths washed out with soap."

Howard laughed. "I've got to put this out for my horses."

"I've got the other two, over in the coulee."

"Hey, wonderful. I was thinking they were gone forever."

"Indians ran them hard but they're still sound—"

"Howard?" Kathren called out from the front of the barn. "You all right?"

"Yeah, back here. He saw your warning."

"Thank God," she said, looking relieved and carrying her dress tail as she hurried inside to join them. "We were worried you might pass us by and run right into them."

"He's returning our horses," Howard said, smiling at her.

"They're over the hill," Slocum explained. "When I saw the underwear, I took heed."

Bright-eyed and fresh-looking, Kathren gave him a warm smile. "We worried something had happened to you."

"No, Able and the girl're fine. Busy mustanging. The two renegades won't bother anyone again."

"What about you?"

"No problem. I've learned the bootleggers are headed south. They don't know the Cayuse renegades are already in custody."

"Why don't we go to the house? Kathren can make some coffee and we can talk. I'll feed the horses and be right there."

"Yes," she said and her face brightened. "Come along."

Slocum nodded and fell in beside her. Howard went out through the side door with his pail of grain. Halfway to the house, she glanced over at him, then in a soft voice said, "It's working out."

Slocum nodded and smiled. "I knew that when I saw your face."

She looked up at the sky and her cheeks flushed. "That obvious?"

"I'm glad for you."

"It will be fun," she said and shook her head as if to clear it. "I don't believe you saw that. You just said that."

"No, Kathren. But still the same, I'm pleased for both of you."

"Where will you go next?"

"Where the wind will take me."

"You will always be in my prayers."

He studied the dark bank of clouds rolling in out of the west. Might be some rain in them. One thing for certain, he could always use some prayers.

Horses returned and with their friendly visit over, an hour before sundown, he left them to ride on. Howard's good arm was looped over her shoulder and she held her man's hand. Slocum nodded at them and set out for the south, shaking out his slicker as thunder began to roll over the land.

Hard raindrops pelted his slicker as he drew near Matty's place. Dogs barked in the night. Matty had new ones, or her old ones had survived. He dismounted at the stoop and the door cracked, a gun barrel shown.

"Who is it?"

"One wet traveler."

"Oh—" The door flew open and she tried to see him through the sheet of runoff from the roof.

"I'll put my horse up?"

"Yes, and come back." A small smile in the corners of her straight mouth, mischief danced in her eyes.

Slocum led the pony off to the corrals. The rain peppered his rubber duster and ran off the brim of his hat. Inside the barn, he listened to the drip of leaks and put the bay in a tie stall, feeding him a can of oats and a forkful of sweet hay. Then he decided to unsaddle him—he doubted that pair of bounty hunters would venture far in this weather.

Another clap of thunder and the flash lighted up the barn's whole interior. He spoke to the pony to calm him as he lifted the saddle and pads off his back. His rig on the partition, he looked aside and saw her standing there, water shining on the yellow raincoat hooded over her.

"How have you been?"

"I guess you don't know about it, but I'm a widow now."

"Oh."

"Merle was shot the last night you were here. Drunk, I guess—some drummer used a derringer on him when he came over to beat him up. Shot him in the heart."

"Have a funeral?"

She shook her head. "They buried him and sent me word."

She wrinkled her nose at the notion. "I reckon he had enough whores there to cry over their financial losses. Hale's coming back in ten days to stay, help me work the place. Him and his boss have some fence to finish."

"You two will make it fine," he said, opening his slicker and holding her tight to him. "Plan on it."

She slung off the raincoat and clung to him. "Tonight we can sleep in my bed in my house."

He laid his cheek on the top of her head and rocked her. Matty was a survivor. Merle's death freed her to prove that.

She raised her face and looked up at him with a frown. "You don't think making love to me is like doing it with a boy, do you?"

"No, Matty. I damn sure don't ever think that."

"Good." She nestled her face against his vest. "You have rocks in this thing?"

"No, just money."

"Good," she said and put her face back on him. "Sure felt lumpy."

The next day he replaced some broken corral rails in between rain showers, made repairs to her pigpen and used flattened tin cans to fix two places where the house roof leaked.

He was seated in a straight-back chair, drinking coffee and listening to the drum of heavier rain in late afternoon.

She worked rolling out pie dough on the dry sink. "Guess we're in for a real rainy spell."

"You dream it?"

"Yes, I did."

"Momma always can dream about rain, Mr. Slocum," the boy Lars said.

"She sure does," Violia added, setting her rag doll in the small bed.

"You kids don't bother him. He don't need to hear your chatter."

"I know," Lars said, "Children are much better seen than heard."

"Why don't you practice it?"

"We will," he said, subdued.

Slocum touseled the boy's hair and smiled at him. "You'll be big enough before you know it."

She looked up and agreed. "Too soon."

After supper, she put the children to sleep in the loft. Only one leak pinged in a pan. "A new one," she complained as they climbed into her bed. They made love under the quilts that felt good, for the night air and storms moving in had dropped the temperature.

Afterward, he kissed her, slipped out of bed and dressed. She got up and fed him another piece of her apple pie and put some bread, cooked pork and dried fruit in a poke for him.

They were quiet moving about in the light of one small flickering candle, so as not to wake the kids. At the door they had a lingering kiss and embrace. Then he pressed ten double eagles in her hand.

"Why this?" she hissed.

"That's for the kids."

She nodded, looking dumbstruck at the coins. "Be careful, Slocum, and you ever ride this way again—come see me."

He nodded and put on his slicker and sodden felt hat. "I will, Matty. I promise."

The dry washes had turned to live creeks to splash through, and the shiny night a constant drum of rain. He reached Whistler's at daybreak and learned from the young store clerk that the two bounty hunters were staying upstairs. Also that Yurbacon and Terry had used the ferry the day before. Slocum gave the boy two dollars to keep his mouth shut about their conversation and headed for the ferry in the half-light of dawn, trying to spear through the overcast.

At the landing, he found the youth asleep. He grabbed him up by the collar and growled in his ear, "I'm back. Get your ass in gear and get me across the river."

"Huh, huh? What's wrong, mister?"

"You told them two bounty hunters where I was." He dragged the boy out of the office toward the barge and tender.

"I swear—"

"Don't lie to me. Get me over there and fast or you'll be salmon food."

"Oh. Yes, sir, I'll hurry. I never—"

Slocum caught the bridle reins and led his horse aboard, keeping an eye on the operator, who was firing the boiler. He stood close by so the boy couldn't do anything funny.

Soon the steam was up and the ferry backing out. When they turned, Slocum heard some shouts. He saw Carter and Ward running pell-mell in the fresh shower and shouting for them to stop.

"Keep sailing," Slocum warned the boy, who looked back bug-eyed from the pilot's wheel.

"But they may shoot us."

"Then we die," he said, knowing a pistol shot would never reach them.

Carter did bust a few caps, but they were in the air to scare them. The ferry went on. Slocum was thinking of all sorts of ways to keep the boy from rushing back and carrying the bounty hunters over. Disable the engine? No, folks needed the ferry. He simply needed to delay their crossing.

At last they struck the bank and the shaking boy secured the ropes to the landing.

"Now what?" he asked.

"Toss all the wood overboard."

"Huh?"

Slocum could see no provisions for fuel on this bank that were loose or accessible. He watched the boy grunt and strain until all his wood was bobbing off down the Snake.

"Now get a bucket and put out the fire in the boiler."

"Huh?"

He drew his Colt, pointed the muzzle at the boy's face and growled, "You heard me. Get busy!"

"Yes, sir."

"When you finish, shovel all that pile of coal overboard, too."

"But it will take—" The bucket of water sloshed in the firebox sizzled, and a gust of steam and smoke came out the doors.

"Exactly." He planned for it to take a half day or more to get the ferry back in service. Perhaps even longer.

All the coal gone, the dejected boy sat on his butt, mopping his face with a red bandanna. "Why didn't you sink it?"

" 'Cause I like your grandfather."

"Huh?"

"You'd never understand. Tell your buddies, Carter and Ward, I'll see them in hell." He stuck his boot toe in the stirrup and mounted up. "You don't hurry back now." And he left.

McGrim sat at his desk and looked up in amazement when Slocum came in his office.

"Figured you were long gone."

"No, I left them two Texans stranded across the Snake. Terry and his partner, Yurbacon, I figure they're back at Terry's cabin right now."

"Let's go get them."

"Fine, but I could use a good night's sleep and a bottle of whiskey."

"How about a meal on me to go with them?"

"Sounds great."

They ate in a private dining room at the hotel: beef steak, fresh potatoes and peas, along with some fine bourbon whiskey. Both men relaxed with cigars after their food.

"Tell me something. How did you know that Lenore would be so receptive to me?" McGrim asked. "She never was before when I called on her."

"A guess."

The lawman shook his head. "I doubt that, but by damn I'm grateful for the word you put in for me."

Slocum shook his head. "She simply came to realize your worth."

"Well, I doubt the hell out of that."

Both men laughed.

Before dawn the two were already saddled and riding west. They reached the canyon and left their horses to go on foot and check out the cabin.

"They may have left, if they learned them Cayuse were all taken back to the reservation by the Army," McGrim said.

"I'd bet they're here."

About then a mule brayed and another honked at him.
Both men grinned and hurried on.

They caught Yurbacon returning from the outhouse and
they surprised Terry coming out the back door when his partner was forced to call for him. McGrim's prisoners shackled
and the mules loaded full with evidence, Slocum shook the
lawman's hand.

"I better get out of here. Tell Carter and Ward I went to
Alaska."

"I won't tell them damn bounty hunters a thing. And you
ever need a favor, don't hesitate to call on me."

Six weeks later, the shadowy street beyond the sidewalk tables was crowded with peddlers shouting about their wares.
Robins and red cardinals sang in the live oak trees. Mourning
doves watered in the gurgling irrigation ditch.

"Firewood," screamed the boy, with his donkey leaden
down with a load of sticks.

"Fresh milk," the man shouted above the bleating goats
around him.

"*Agua! Agua!*"

"What are your reading about?" she asked, coming over
and setting down his coffee.

He lowered the paper and smiled up at the shapely se-
ñorita, Arnetta Santiago. Memories of the night before with
her in bed were still sharply etched in his mind. The aroma
of her heady perfume filled the cool morning air. "They've
had a record early snowfall in eastern Washington and
Oregon."

"That is bad?"

He hugged her hip with one arm and laughed. "No, my
darling. But it will be good for the next wheat crop."

She looked at him with a frown; then they both laughed.

He shook his head and blew on the hot coffee. He could
only hope that Carter and Ward froze their asses and other
body parts off up there in the deep white stuff.

Watch for

SLOCUM AND THE BAD-NEWS BROTHERS

302nd novel in the exciting SLOCUM series
from Jove

Coming in April!